Also by **VALERIE HOBBS**

Minnie McClary Speaks Her Mind

The Last Best Days of Summer

Sheep

Anything but Ordinary

Defiance

*Letting Go of Bobby James, or
How I Found My Self of Steam*

Stefan's Story

Sonny's War

Tender

Charlie's Run

Carolina Crow Girl

WOLF

VALERIE HOBBS

WoLF

FRANCES FOSTER BOOKS

FARRAR STRAUS GIROUX

NEW YORK

Farrar Straus Giroux Books for Young Readers
175 Fifth Avenue, New York 10010

Text copyright © 2013 by Valerie Hobbs
Printed in the United States of America
by RR Donnelley & Sons Company, Harrisonburg, Virginia
Designed by Andrew Arnold
First edition, 2013
1   3   5   7   9   10   8   6   4   2

mackids.com

Library of Congress Cataloging-in-Publication Data
Hobbs, Valerie.
    Wolf / Valerie Hobbs. — First edition.
       pages cm
    Sequel to: Sheep.
    Summary: Jack has found a home and a purpose on a farm, keeping a
flock of sheep safe from coyotes and training pups to do the same, but now
he and his boy, Luke, must face a rabid wolf that threatens them all.
    ISBN 978-0-374-31575-7 (hardback)
    ISBN 978-0-374-31576-4 (e-book)
    1. Border collie—Juvenile fiction.   [1. Border collie—Fiction.
2. Dogs—Fiction.   3. Sheep—Fiction.   4. Wolves—Fiction.
5. Rabies—Fiction.   6. Adventure and adventurers—Fiction.]   I. Title.

PZ10.3.H6463Wol 2013
[Fic]—dc23

                                                        2013009698

Farrar Straus Giroux Books for Young Readers may be purchased for business
or promotional use. For information on bulk purchases please contact
Macmillan Corporate and Premium Sales Department at (800) 221-7945 x5442
or by email at specialmarkets@macmillan.com.

For my grandsons, Diego and Rafael Salgado

WOLF

The lone gray wolf counted his journey in moons. Three moons since his last big kill, two since his last sighting of man. How many moons since the day he left his pack, he no longer knew. He simply moved on.

All around him the world changed and kept changing. Rock-strewn hills became grassy slopes. Thick woods became open field. He stopped to examine the sharp barbs of his first fence, then journeyed on again, driven by hunger that clung like a shadow, pulling him closer to the habitats of man, and danger.

He had not left his pack willingly. He had been nudged, then forced. There came a time when staying was harder than leaving. He had to go. A grown male in his prime must make his own way. He must find a mate, not within his pack but somewhere beyond.

Leaving the territory of his birth, he had expected to encounter more of his kind. To fight them for food, for territory, for a female. But he had found none. He was lonely, a feeling so unfamiliar that at first he confused it with hunger.

But it was deeper than hunger and lived inside him like a second self.

From time to time, he would stop and look back at the gray shape of the mountains growing ever smaller in the distance. Home. The alpha pair that had reared him. Warmth and safety. But he could not return to that place. They would not welcome him. For better or worse, he belonged to this bigger world now.

He had come at last into the flatlands, fields that stretched to the limits of his vision. Food was abundant. He had only to wait for a small furry head to emerge from a burrow. Then a single clamp of his powerful jaws and the creature was his.

But the wolf preferred the woods, where he could blend in, his coat the colors of tree bark. Kills were more difficult here. His prey could climb or fly or slither out of reach, but he could rest when he needed to without having to be on guard.

Somehow he knew that his journey was coming to an end. He had not found a mate. He was weary and his spirits no longer lifted with the sun's rising.

Near the end of the moon's journey, he hunted down a large rodent that was quick and, in the end, vicious. It snarled and fought and sank its teeth deep into the wolf's chest before he managed to shake it off. Angry with his kill and with himself, he tore the rodent apart and ate it down to the last small bone.

As long as he could kill, he could eat, and as long as he could eat, he could survive. For now that was enough. The rest would come when it came, or would not.

1

JACK AWOKE FROM HIS DREAM with his back legs still running. A horrible man with a whip had been chasing him and Jack had run in terrified circles around and around inside a barn, unable to escape.

What a relief it was to open his eyes to the place where he was loved and not in Billy's Big and Happy Circus, where he had barely escaped with his life years ago.

Now his life here was perfect, except for the one thing that pestered him like a nasty flea: he was growing old. Or maybe he was already old. Getting up in the morning from his rug by the side of Luke's bed was no longer easy, not even for a Border collie. His legs were stiff. In cold weather they ached. Sometimes, to his embarrassment, he would grunt a little in pain.

Still, he always awoke before Luke, who liked to sleep in. Jack would poke his cold nose under the blankets, searching for just the right spot to make Luke squirm. "Aw, Jack," Luke would groan. "Can't you let a guy sleep?"

But Jack's nose wasn't needed to get his best friend

out of bed this morning. The minute Luke's eyes opened, his feet hit the floor and he was climbing into his work clothes.

"You know what, Jack?" Luke said, pulling on his boots. "It's my birthday. I'm finally a teenager. Isn't that great?"

Jack didn't see the difference. Luke had never acted much like a kid, and he looked the same as always, only taller. He liked his sleep—who didn't? But when it came to doing his chores he never let his family down.

It was the same for Jack. He would rather die than disappoint Luke.

This morning, Jack bounced along on Luke's happy mood. They got through their chores in record time, feeding the dogs, the cats, and milking Bertha the kicking cow.

A bright ball of sun was peeking into the world, spreading warmth through Jack's bones. A soft breeze ruffled his fur. He followed Luke out to the barn, and when he saw Luke grab his saddle, he began rounding up the two-year-olds.

Today Jack was determined not to go easy on them. He would put them through their trials and expect perfection. He needed to see which of them could take over when he retired.

He didn't want to retire. The thought of staying behind while the younger dogs did the job he was born to do troubled him, but it was irresponsible not to have someone ready to step in. His job now was to find that dog and train him to lead. He would do it as he'd done every job he was ever given, to the best of his ability.

He gave his signal bark and Sarge came at once. Sarge, a two-year-old, was a good collie, strong and responsible. He wasn't quick, and his senses were not as sharp as they should be, but he was a dog Jack could count on for backup when he needed it.

He touched noses with Sarge and barked his signal again.

Casey and Freckles came around the corner of the barn together. With their nearly identical white faces, they were impossible to tell apart when they were born, at least for Luke, who couldn't pick them out by smell alone. It wasn't until they began to wobble around at about three weeks that the spots on Freckles's snout began to darken and gave her the name she was called by.

He and the three two-year-olds waited outside the barn until Luke climbed into the saddle. "Ready, Jack?"

Jack's answering woof put boy and horse into motion. Sarge, Casey, and Freckles set off behind them. Jack was about to take his place at the end when he heard a familiar bark and turned. There was Jackie racing as fast as

her year-old legs would carry her, heading straight toward him.

What was she doing? He had told her that she was not
to come. And here she was disobeying him. But she was
his favorite and she knew it. Stopping just short of her
grandfather, her eyes as filled with excitement as Luke's
were this morning, she woofed.

He didn't answer.

She ran three circles around him, then stopped and
waited, panting, her tail wagging eagerly. Her face with
its classic black mask was so like his own. *Let me come,
let me come,* she pleaded.

Freckles bumped Jackie's rump, hard. Casey gave her
a low growl.

But Jackie wouldn't back down, and Jack finally
gave in.

It was more than love that made his decision. Jackie
had talent. More than any pup he'd ever known. He supposed her mother had something to do with it. Callie
was one smart female and, like Jack himself, a prizewin-
ning herder. But it was not only that. Jackie's instincts
were strong and unfailing, so like his own.

He gave Jackie his no-nonsense look and ordered her
to stay right on his heels. Any misbehaving and it was
back to the barn. She fell into step behind him, stopping
only to sniff the ground when her nose made her do it.

Jackie was thrilled to be out among the sheep, and Jack remembered exactly how that felt. He would let her wander for a while, then give her a taste of sheepherding. How much trouble could a yearling pup get into anyway?

The wolf was growing weary and his pace had slowed. Instinct told him that he must stay strong or he would be taken down like prey.

His wound from the rodent bite had begun to fester and itch. He tried to put it out of his mind, but he could not.

When at last he saw in the distance a swath of thick trees, his spirits lifted. He loped ahead until the woods surrounded him. There he ate whatever he could find, squirrels, rabbits, a fat juicy snake.

Revived, he moved on through the woods and found a field again, an open, grass-covered field stretched out beneath a deep blue sky.

And prey! Prey he had never seen the likes of. Slow prey. Fat and thickly furred, they waited to be taken down. The wolf raised his snout. Instinct was strong. He needed to howl. He wanted to call his pack to the feast, though he knew they would not come. They would not even hear him, and he would give himself away.

On his haunches, he was about to make his move when the canines appeared. Too small to be wolves, they were as agile and quick as the fat prey were slow. If one of the prey wandered from its kind, a canine was there on the spot to bring it back.

As he watched from behind a tree, the wolf could see that the alpha canine had age bearing down upon him. The young one who resembled the alpha in color and markings was faster. She looked to the old one for approval. The two touched noses, and the young one ran off again.

An unfamiliar feeling arose in the wolf. This, too, he tried to ignore, but it was as if something had stuck to his paw that he could not shake off. It had made for a restless sleep, this feeling he had no name for.

He had no kind. No one to greet with the touching of noses and rubs and licks. No one to return to. He was alone. He might always be.

2

JACK FOLLOWED THE SHEEP, checking for the patches of paint on their flanks that identified them. When Old Sally stopped at a patch of sparse grass, all the sheep pushed in. It had been a dry year. Jack could feel the worry that fell over the ranch each night like darkness. The sheep needed nourishment to produce the fine wool that Olaf and Katrin were known for. Hay could be bought, but there was little money to spare.

Another dry year or two might ruin them.

Jack remembered all too well the last days at his birth ranch and worried as much as anybody. First came drought, then fire, then the selling of animals, down to the last pup. In no time, it seemed, he had gone from pet shop to a little girl's baby carriage, and when he could stand no more he hit the road. That was where he met his great friend, the Goat Man, and when the Goat Man was no more, all the others: some good, like Hollerin; some not-so-good, like Snatch; and some downright evil, like Billy from the circus. Then, best of all, came Luke, who needed a home as much as he did, and Olaf and Katrin, who took them in.

But that was the past. Today, like any other good day, there was work to do. Jack put the dogs through their paces, culling a half dozen sheep from the flock, then neatly returning them. Freckles was best at this, so Jack sent Jackie off with her. The sheep were annoyed but obedient. But when Jackie threatened to nip Old Sally's leg, she got one of the ewe's meanest looks.

Jackie backed off, her feelings hurt.

Old Sally demanded respect. She and Jack had built something almost like a friendship over the years. She would help him out with the lambs, if he would leave her alone. She gave him a baleful look now as if to say, *Who is this whippersnapper you've brought out today? Tell it to back off.*

Jackie backed off. Old Sally was twice her size and twice as mean as any sheep she'd met so far.

Luke was out riding the perimeter. There had been talk of coyotes, but so far it had been just that: talk. Nobody had seen one for several months. Still, you had to watch for them. Drought brought the coyotes closer in, and their hunger made them brave. In packs, they could easily pick off the younger or weaker sheep. Olaf and Katrin had lost two sheep to coyotes, both in Jack's first year with them.

It had been his fault, though nobody blamed him.

Jack had never before seen a coyote, and if he had, might have thought it was just some long-legged, strange-stepping dog. But he blamed himself. Not since that first year had another sheep been lost on his watch.

He vowed there never would be.

Jack watched the hills now. Through eyes that had lost a little of their sharpness, he scanned the trees at the edge of the woods. The coyotes, if they attacked, would come from there. Unless they came in great numbers, Jack was confident that he and the dogs could deal with them. But no coyotes appeared. Jack had time to run the dogs through several more drills before Luke came riding back.

"Let's head in," he said, to Jack's surprise. The sun was still high. "I don't want to miss my party!"

So that was the reason for Luke's happy mood. He was going to have a birthday party. Jack figured it would be like all the parties in the years before, with lots of food and noise. Jack could sneak in a nap and maybe a few extra treats. He rounded up the dogs and they fell in line behind him.

All but Jackie.

Putting Sarge in the lead, Jack went back for Jackie. He had to admit that she'd done well today. Her feints had improved and all morning she kept her focus where it needed to be: on the job.

Where was she now?

He sent her a sharp bark and, when it wasn't returned, set off to find her.

Jackie was not among the sheep. Jack went up one of the hills to get an overview of the field and the thin stream that had once been a river at the far end.

She was not at the water. She was not anywhere to be seen.

His errant granddaughter could only be in one other place: the woods.

Jack, worried now, raced down the hill and across the field. If that silly darned pup had gone deep into the woods . . .

At the edge of the trees, he barked again. An answering bark came from within, not far away but far enough. Jack plunged in, leaves and twigs snapping beneath the pads of his feet. A myriad of odors assaulted his nose: dry leaves, decay, dung beetles, urine.

He stopped only long enough to sniff the base of a tree. Coyote? He couldn't be certain. The scent was stronger, more acrid, and, well, just *different*. There was something wrong with this animal. Some sickness.

He barked again and Jackie came bounding through the trees, her coat full of stickers and dry leaves. "Big feet!" she said excitedly. "I saw a snake and a bird that was dead and a dog with giant feet!"

He didn't have to speak to let her know how much

trouble she was in. They ran side by side, Jack breathing hard and trying not to show it, while Jackie kept on about the dog with the giant feet.

He finally told her to knock it off. Dogs didn't have giant feet. Neither, for that matter, did coyotes. She was seeing things. The woods had a spooky way of doing that to you.

When they reached the barn, he sent Jackie inside to spend the rest of the day. She obeyed, her tail between her legs.

Giant feet. Jack's heart suddenly felt heavy. If Jackie's imagination was greater than her judgment, he might have to reevaluate her worth as a herding dog.

It was only at that moment, leaving Jackie behind in the barn, that Jack realized what he'd had in mind for her all along. He had wanted her to prove not only to himself but to the others that she was fit to lead. Now that hope might be dashed.

Giant feet. He almost wished she hadn't told him.

Caught up in his disappointment, Jack didn't recall the urine mark in the woods until dinner. He had guessed that a coyote left that strange mark. Now he still wasn't sure, but if not a coyote, what could it be?

3

LUKE'S PARTY was in full swing. Whole families from neighboring ranches had come, and the house was stuffed with people. In the four years since Luke and Jack had been adopted, this was Luke's biggest birthday party yet. Before Olaf and Katrin, he'd never had a party, and no real family at all.

Jack zigzagged his way through dozens of legs until he found Mandy Cross. She was sitting on the floor, wearing her worn jeans and a wrinkled shirt. Her hair looked like the back end of Banner, her horse, but her smile was sweet and her touch gentle. Of all Luke's friends, Mandy was Jack's favorite. Jack settled himself beside her.

"Happy birthday to you! Happy birthday to you!" Luke blew out the candles on his triple-layer chocolate cake and everybody cheered.

"Open your presents, Luke," said Cece, Mandy's older sister, fluffing her blond ringlets. "Mine first, please." She handed Luke a small, flat package tied with a yellow bow that matched her sundress and the bow in her hair.

A blush spread over Luke's cheeks and he ducked his head. Muttering a thanks, he tore the paper off. Inside was a woven yellow friendship bracelet, the kind the girls made for each other.

"Uh, thanks," said Luke, and quickly set the bracelet aside.

"Oh! You don't like it!" Tears sprang into Cece's blue eyes. "I was afraid of that."

"No! It's . . . nice," Luke said, blushing all the more.

"It won't hurt you to wear it," said Cece's father, big Curtis Cross. "Put it on!"

Frowning, Luke slipped the bracelet on his wrist.

When cheers went up, Luke looked like he wanted to fall through the floor.

Only Jack understood how uncomfortable his best friend was. The bracelet was too much like the halter Jack had been forced to wear in that terrible circus long ago. The bracelet was only made of string, but its intention was the same: to claim a fellow and hold him down.

By the look on Mandy's face, Jack could tell she didn't like that bracelet either. Every now and then, she'd sneak a look at Luke and her cheeks would redden.

Jack had seen this same behavior in dogs, only without all the changing of face color. It was clear to him that both Cece and Mandy wanted to be Luke's mate. Mandy with her sweet, shy smile was Jack's choice, but

Cece was the alpha dog. Around her, Luke didn't have a choice: it was her or no one.

A cloud of weariness settled over Jack. He laid his snout in Mandy's lap. She smiled and smoothed her soft hand over his head until his eyelids fluttered and shut.

". . . coyotes . . ."

Jack caught only that one word and his eyes sprang open.

"Saw one loping across my land just the other evening, right about sunset," said Curtis Cross. "I got it in my sights, pulled off a shot, and, I swear, the thing flat out disappeared. Just like that!" He snapped his fingers.

Olaf and another neighbor, a big, beefy man they called Pinky, all started laughing. "You're losing it, Curt," Pinky teased. "You can't shoot straight, that's all."

But Jack knew better. He had seen the very thing Curtis Cross had described. Coyotes were the strangest creatures. In the blink of an eye they could turn into air. Jack didn't know how they did it—one minute the coyotes were there, the next they were gone. It was spooky.

The cake was cut into slices and passed around. Jack drifted off to sleep, but not before he heard the men arguing about guns. Olaf was what Curtis called a "pacifist." The rifle that hung over the fireplace was only to protect his family should someone threaten them. He could not bring himself to kill an animal.

"The coyotes come and you're going to have to pick them off, like it or not," said Curtis Cross. "You can't ask us to be saving your flock as well as our own."

"And I won't," said Olaf. "The dogs and I will take care of the coyotes, same as we always have."

"Maybe so, maybe not," said Curtis Cross, but he'd looked right at Jack as if he were counting the white hairs on Jack's snout. He didn't believe Jack was up to the job, not anymore, and Pinky probably thought the same thing. Only Olaf and Luke held on to their stubborn belief in Jack.

He would not let them down.

The party broke up, Katrin reminding Cece and Mandy that they as well as Luke would be writing an essay in their homeschool class on Monday. Luke made a face. Cece giggled. Katrin, their English teacher, was pretty easy on them. They could probably talk her into putting off the essay.

Mrs. Cross was tougher. If you didn't study your biology, you got extra homework and no snack. But their toughest teacher was Mr. Cross, who taught them history and what he called "the nuts and bolts of living." If you didn't do the homework he assigned, you got to weed his vegetable garden.

Katrin, Olaf, and Luke followed their guests into the yard to say goodbye. The moon was full, the air warm and still. Mandy smiled shyly at Luke. Cece whispered something in his ear. Jack stuck his nose under Luke's hand to remind him who his real best friend was. Luke let his hand rest on Jack's head.

"Looks like nice weather for the county fair tomorrow," said Olaf.

"Yep," said Curtis Cross. "Adele has been baking pies all day. She's counting on first place this year."

"So are we. Aren't we, Jack?" said Luke. On a wall in Luke's room hung the three first-place ribbons Jack had won in the county fair herding trials.

"Don't be too sure," said Pinky. "Jack's not the dog he was, young man. Our Buster's sure to win this year."

"We'll see about that," said Luke, his voice filled with pride. Jack shrank a little beneath Luke's hand. He knew Pinky was right. He didn't have the speed or the agility he used to have. But Luke had stars in his eyes again and Jack could not bear to let him down.

And he wouldn't! Buster was young and quick, but he didn't have the experience that Jack had. Jack would get that ribbon one more time.

Just then, from across the dark fields, came the bone-chilling sound of a coyote pack. *Yip-yip harrooo! Yip-yip harrooo!* Luke looked over at Olaf, whose eyes held a world of worry.

"If I were you," said Pinky, "I'd clean that old gun before you go after them coyotes. How long's it been since you shot that thing anyway?"

Olaf shrugged. "Long time," he said, kicking his boot through the dust.

Curtis Cross shook his head. "Get yourself a decent gun and be ready to use it," he said. "That's my advice to you!" He turned on his heel and stomped off.

Yip-yip! went the coyotes. *Harrooo!*

On a hill in the distance, silhouetted against the full moon, a coyote raised its head and howled again. *Harrooo! Harrooo!*

Jack's hackles went up. Then, almost out of hearing, he heard another sound, a lone howl that made his blood turn cold.

Within the territory that he had marked well, the wolf had caught and killed a large feline. It lay beneath his paw now, its eyes losing their luster, its heart stopped. The spotted feline had been smart and quick. It had leapt for a tree, and the wolf had snatched it in midair.

He did not like the taste of this animal, but it was food. It filled his belly. He ate all but the skull and the larger bones. He slept with the singing of the wind through the trees and dreamed of his home.

Waking in the morning, he thought at once about the fat prey and made his way through the trees to the open field. The feline had settled badly in his stomach and he did not feel well.

He had not felt right since the rodent bite. His wound still would not heal. His dreams were disturbed by strange sounds and images. Piercing barks and flashing teeth, men with noisy sticks. At times he dreamed while awake. He was not himself. The furry prey across the field and halfway up the slope beyond did not excite him as they had the day before.

And there was man. Riding slowly upon tall, four-legged animals, man seemed to be guarding the prey. But the canines did all of the work, racing at top speed even when they didn't need to. The prey were docile, easily controlled.

When did the canines kill and eat the prey? This was what the wolf wondered. He could not understand why they would wait. It must be that man, and not canine, was alpha. If that was so, man would decide when the canines could eat.

Waiting for his stomach to settle, the wolf groomed himself and licked at his wound.

4

COUNTY FAIR DAY meant baths.

Bummer.

Jack sat unhappily but patiently in the soapy tub watching Olaf pour a bucket of water over Jackie's head. Jackie squealed and tried to bolt. "Hold on!" said Olaf. "You can shake yourself silly in a minute."

"Behave," ordered Jack in a low growl.

Jackie whined and shook.

"You sure you want to bring her along?" said Luke. "She's pretty skittish."

Olaf squeezed Jackie's snout and made her look at him. "You'll be a good girl, won't you?"

Jackie sneezed in his face.

"You little stinker!" said Olaf, dumping a second pail of water over her head.

Jack hoped Luke would change Olaf's mind about taking Jackie. Jackie was young and unpredictable. When she wasn't herding, every smell sent her off in a different direction. She'd follow a hawk into the air if she could, or run down a bumblebee. Fair day was bad enough without having to watch a silly, half-grown pup. He had his own worries to contend with.

Luke filled the pail. Jack steeled himself as the cold water splashed over his head.

"She needs to see what trials are all about," said Olaf. "She'll get to see Jack win his ribbon."

Jack looked up at Luke, trying to read his eyes. Doubt came creeping into him like thick morning fog. Could he really win this year? Was he the only one who noticed how slow he'd become? He still knew sheepherding better than any dog on any farm, but lately his legs wouldn't listen to his brain, or his brain would wander off. Without warning, it would start thinking about something Not Sheep.

Losing focus was the absolute worst thing that could happen to a sheepherding dog. It would finish him. He would spend the rest of his days on his rug under the table feeling sorry for himself.

He might as well *be* the rug.

Luke rubbed Jack all over with a sun-warmed towel, nothing but love and belief in his eyes. When Jack was dry, Luke brushed him until his coat shone.

"You're a handsome dude," said Luke, as he always said when all Jack's good smells of himself had been washed away. Jack could never understand why his human friends detested their own good smells so much. They scrubbed themselves with soap, sprayed stuff under their arms, then doused themselves with perfume. You could smell them long before they got to you, and they didn't smell good.

Katrin came out with a wrapped-up pie and climbed into the pickup. Last year her peach pie had won second place and a small ribbon. This year she was hoping for the big ribbon.

Ribbons! What was so exciting about a piece of ribbon? But Jack knew. It was what the ribbon meant: that you were the best. Not second or third best, but the very best, the Top Dog.

Olaf lowered the tailgate for Jack and Jackie. Luke would ride to the fair on Cheyenne, but the dogs were not to get dirty again. And Jack needed to save his energy for the trials.

Today they would come home with two big shiny ribbons. Katrin's would hang in the kitchen next to the second-place one from last year. Jack's would go next to the other big ribbons on Luke's wall.

Jack got a whiff of doubt fog and shook it out of his head.

Sheepherding trials. He wished they'd never been invented. Wasn't it enough for a dog to do his job? Did he have to show off, too?

Jack lay down in the bed of the truck, his snout on

his paws, remembering his last trials. Or the ones before. They were all mixed up in his mind. What he remembered best was the excitement in Luke's eyes and the pride when Jack won. *And* the steak he got for dinner, a whole steak just for him.

But what if he lost? No steak?

Would Luke cry? That was the worst thing Jack could imagine. The last time Luke cried, he had broken a toe, and it broke Jack's heart. Jack had licked and licked the tears from Luke's face but they just kept coming like a leaking water faucet. If Jack lost today, Luke wouldn't cry, not in front of the girls, but he might cry in his bed at night or in his closet.

How terrible that would be!

Jack leapt to his feet. He had to stop worrying about losing. He wasn't going to lose. He never lost.

Jackie bounded from one side of the truck bed to the other. *Where's the fair? What's a fair? Are we there yet?*

"Behave," said Jack. "We'll be there soon enough."

But Jackie could not keep still. Her ears were perked, her eyes wide with excitement, her tail wagging like crazy. And she didn't even know what a fair was!

They saw the big wheel from a long way off. Set in the center of all the booths, its job was to lift people into the air and spin them around while they screamed. The first time Jack saw the wheel, whose name was Ferris, he must have looked just as wide-eyed and disbelieving as Jackie did now. Why would a person get onto a contraption like that? But Luke, a smart person, the smartest person Jack knew, rode the thing every year. There had to be something to it.

Jack explained the wheel to Jackie as best he could, but he could see she wasn't going to get it either. There were just some things a dog would never understand. Ferris was one of them.

Olaf parked the pickup in a big field between two other trucks, one of them Pinky's. Up from the bed of Pinky's truck came Buster's big black and white head. Before Pinky could lower the tailgate, Buster leapt cleanly over the side, landing lightly on the grass.

Show-off.

Olaf lowered the tailgate. Jackie bounded out. Jack stepped down as any dog with a shred of dignity would. But Buster wasn't looking. He was halfway across the field, bouncing along beside Pinky, ready for the sheep.

Jack felt like crawling under the truck for a nice, long nap. Instead, he gave himself a good hard shake. He remembered how it was to feel like Buster and Jackie. He wished he could feel that kind of excitement today. He would win today, he always did. He just wished he could be more excited about it.

As they headed across the field, a balloon on a long

string danced up and up into a clear blue sky. No chance of rain. No chance the trials would be called off. The air was filled with a mixture of smells—hot dogs, popcorn, sticky apples, chicken manure, sheep, and his favorite treat, barbecued ribs.

Jackie kept racing ahead and running back again. *Is this the fair? Are we there? Where are the sheep?*

Jack had told her as much as she needed to know about the fair. There were animals and games and contests and lots of food and, of course, the sheepherding trials. He told Jackie the most important thing: she needed to behave herself. If she acted up or disobeyed, no more fairs for her.

Which was pretty much an empty threat. If she proved to be as quick with the sheep as she'd been the other day, she would be in the trials as soon as next year.

So Olaf had been right to bring her along, even though Jack would have to keep his eye on her the whole time.

Well, not the whole time. There were the trials, after all.

And he began to worry again.

"There's Luke," said Olaf. "He must have taken the shortcut."

Luke rode up and dismounted. Jack pushed his snout into Luke's hand.

"Where are Mandy and Cece?" said Katrin.

Luke shrugged. "Still coming, I guess. Girls are slow."

"On a younger horse, Mandy could outrun you any day of the week," said Katrin. "And you know it."

Luke laughed. "Well, not today."

Olaf shook his head. "That girl needs a good horse."

"She doesn't want another horse," said Luke. "She and Banner grew up together."

Katrin cupped one hand over her eyes to shade them. Resting on her other hand was the peach pie. Jack hated that pie. It didn't have to do anything to win a ribbon but sit on a table.

"I'm going to go drop off this pie," said Katrin. "When do the trials start?"

"Ten o'clock," said Olaf.

"Hey, guys! Wait up!" Luke hurried ahead to join Rafa and Tom, his two friends who went to the public school.

Jack liked Rafa and Tom. They stooped to pet Jackie and him the way boys always did, with a lot of thumping and neck scratching. They kept calling Jack "Champ" and "the winner."

It was like the trials were over and he'd already won.

The dogs followed the boys to a booth where they could win stuff for shooting cans off a shelf. Tom got a prize and offered it to Jack, who turned up his nose. He didn't want to be seen with a fuzzy green frog in his mouth. But Jackie did. At least until she tore its head off.

Jack growled under his breath. *Behave.*

"But—"

"Behave!" he said.

She looked behind him and her ears went up. Jack turned and saw what had gotten Jackie's attention. A door had come loose on a big wire cage and a flock of hens were making a run for it, squawking and racing in all directions.

Faster than Jack could issue a warning, Jackie shot off after them. Feathers and dust flew into the air as Jackie skidded to a stop. Surrounded by terrified chickens, she looked lost and confused. Then her herding instincts took over. Racing around to confront the boldest hen, she laid herself down and glared. The hen leaned over and pecked Jackie's head. Jackie raced to confront another wandering chicken, who leapt into the air squawking as if she'd been shot. Undaunted, Jackie raced back and forth, flattening herself, then jumping to her feet to race again, sheepherding to the best of her ability.

But chickens weren't sheep. They hardly knew what they were. Squawking frantically, all they could do was flap their wings and run in circles. Jackie pinned one under her paw but the second she let the hen go, she was up and running again.

The boys howled as if they'd never seen anything so funny. "Get 'em, Jackie!" yelled Rafa.

Jack watched about all he could take. Here was the dog he thought might succeed him standing in the middle of a pack of crazy chickens with a feather on her nose. Where was her dignity? She was a Border collie! Jack felt like crawling under a booth.

He called Jackie off. She came to him with her tail dragging. Her face said it all: *What did I do wrong?*

"Chickens are not for herding," said Jack in his sternest voice.

She cocked her head. "Then what are they for?"

"Eating," he said.

Her eyes lit up. "Eating?"

"People eat them, not dogs," said Jack. "Who gave you the order to herd those chickens, Jackie?"

She couldn't look him in the eye. "Nobody."

"Do you like this fair?" he said.

Her head came up and she bounced on all fours, her tail on triple-speed. "Yes! Yes!"

Jack gave her the stare he saved for only the worst sheep. "Well, this is your last one unless you behave," he said.

Her tail drooped. "But I thought I was helping!" she said. She walked along beside her grandfather like she'd been shot through the heart.

5

JACK SAW MANDY AND CECE long before the
boys even noticed them. They were walking ahead eating the fluffy stuff that came on sticks.

"Hey, isn't that your girlfriend?" said Rafa, pointing at
Cece.

Luke frowned. "She's not my girlfriend. Quit calling
her that. She's a neighbor, that's all. Isn't that right,
Jack?"

Jack wagged his tail in agreement.

"See?" said Luke.

Tom raised an eyebrow. "Jack's a cool dog and all," he
said, "but he doesn't understand every single thing you
say, Luke. That's bogus."

"He doesn't?" said Luke. "Watch this."

They all stopped while Luke lifted Jack's snout, looking straight into his eyes. "Bring me the best girl," he
said.

Now it was true that Jack didn't understand every
word Luke said, but he sure knew "best." Whenever
Luke or Olaf wanted to show off one of the sheep, they'd

ask Jack to bring the "best" one. Jack would cull out one with good thick wool, what they called a "high-quality" animal.

Jack knew a high-quality animal when he saw one, and he knew the word "girl." Racing ahead, he slipped between Cece and Mandy and began herding Mandy back to Luke.

"Jack!" Mandy laughed. "What are you doing?" Jack had her by the pants leg and began tugging her over to Luke.

"What's going on?" said Cece.

Rafa was laughing so hard he could barely get the words out. "Luke told Jack to get the best—"

"Shut *up*!" said Luke. "Jack was just messing around, that's all!"

"The best what?" said Cece.

Luke's face was bright red. Sweat beads lined his upper lip. "The best— I don't know! Sheep!" he cried, throwing his hands in the air.

Cece stuck her fists on her hips and frowned. Mandy started to giggle.

"*Boys*," said Cece. "They never grow up. Come on, Mandy. We've got better things to do than hang out with stupid boys."

The boys couldn't stop laughing. "Stop!" cried Tom. "I'm going to bust a gut!"

Rafa was all bent over, grabbing his side. "Ow!" he cried. "Ow!"

"The best *sheep*!" howled Tom.

"I couldn't think!" said Luke when the girls were gone. "Cece just, I don't *know*, she scares me!"

"She's got the hots for you, lover boy!" said Rafa.

"Some lover boy!" said Tom. "He calls the girls sheep!"

Luke suddenly went still and his eyes widened. "What time is it?"

Tom took out his phone. "Nine forty-eight."

"Whoa!" cried Luke. "It's almost time for trials. Come on!"

They raced through the fairgrounds, past all the colorful booths that Jackie wanted to explore, dodging strollers and wheelchairs. "Hurry!" urged Luke.

They got to the fenced-off stretch of field just in time for the first trial. Jack recognized the female named Lucy, who was waiting to herd. He'd had his eye on her once, a healthy black Border collie with a white-tipped tail. They'd have made some fine pups if they'd been given the chance.

The gate swung open. The five sheep trotted out nicely enough but soon began to wander. It looked to Jack like Lucy had a good bunch to herd, dumb and docile. At a signal from her handler, she began her outrun.

Lucy responded well to her handler's whistle, a short

or long low blast, or a high low high. She would drop to the ground, perfectly still, or leap to her feet and be off at a run. But toward the end of her trial, when she was supposed to separate two sheep from three, she blew it. Off she went with four sheep, leaving the fifth to wander in circles.

Lucy realized her mistake at once, but it was too late. No ribbon for her.

Jack felt sorry for Lucy as she left the field, her tail tucked. He hoped her handler wouldn't be too hard on her. Separating sheep wasn't easy. You had to know how to count.

Jack was up fifth. Three more trials to sit through as his heart did a steady, low thump in his chest. Watching Lucy had eased him a bit. There wasn't a thing she was asked to do that he couldn't do better.

Another all-black Border collie was next, a male named Shyster. Like Jack, he had some gray hairs on his snout. His handler's voice was piercing as any whistle. "Come-bye!" she called, and the collie, keeping the right distance from the sheep, began flanking them. "Stand!" The collie slowed, then quickly checked with his handler and stopped still.

Shyster's handler frowned. Something between them wasn't right. They didn't have their signals down. It happened once more. But at the end of his trial, the collie neatly separated one sheep from the five, put them back together, and herded them all into the pen. Jack was glad for him then. Shyster wouldn't win, but he'd done the hardest thing.

Jack began to wonder why he'd been so worried, especially when the next collie nipped a sheep's leg to keep it in line. Nipping showed a complete lack of skill. You had to do it sometimes, but always you knew you could have held your temper in check. You could have intimidated the sheep with a look. If the sheep knew who was boss, they obeyed. Easy as that.

Buster was next. Jack couldn't help but notice what a fine-looking, long-legged Border collie he was. His black-and-white coat was thick and shiny. Intelligence shone in his eyes. He was ready and eager to go.

Pinky swung open the gate to the letting-out pen. Out came four nervous-looking sheep and one straggler. Buster wasted no time going out in a wide run as he was ordered to. Coming in behind the sheep, he expertly herded them toward Pinky.

When the straggler tried to make a move, Buster gave him the old sheep-eye and back he went.

"He's good," said Luke. "I like the way he moves."

Jack felt like he'd swallowed a piece of bone that was poking a hole in his stomach. He shifted away from Luke.

I like the way he moves.

Jack looked up at Luke, who was still watching Buster. *You used to like the way I moved, too. Remember?*

Jack could feel the audience waiting for the final trick, when Buster would have to separate, regather, and pen the sheep. He could only hope that Buster didn't know how to count.

Pinky gave the order. Without a second's hesitation, Buster neatly separated two sheep from three and drove both groups into the pen. Applause broke out in the stands like claps of thunder.

"Well, there goes that ribbon," said Tom with a sigh.

"Don't be so sure," said Rafa. "The champ's up next."

"That's right," said Luke, patting Jack's rump. "Ready, Jack?"

Jack put everything he had into an answering yip. He'd be faster than Buster. He'd be perfect. He'd been perfect before when the pressure was on. And it sure was now.

"Okay, boy, let's go!"

With his head high, Jack looked across the field to where the sheep were waiting in their pen like sheep always did. As if they didn't know what they were waiting for. Food? Freedom? Shearing? They just milled around inside the pen across the field and they waited.

Jack gave them a once-over. Four were young and nervous. One was a ewe about the age of Old Sally. Jack could see by the look in her eye that she meant to be trouble.

The gate opened and the sheep began to amble out.

At Luke's command, Jack began his outrun, going wider as he approached the sheep, then moving in closer but not so close as to spook them.

He had it down. He knew how to do this. He had worried himself over nothing. As he began to herd the sheep straight toward Luke, something inside him settled. His legs felt strong and sure. When the ewe tried to make her move, Jack eyed her back into place. In went the sheep through the first set of gates.

Scattered applause. "You go, Jack!" cried Tom.

On the crossdrive, the ewe began acting up again. She didn't want to go straight across the field to the other gates. She kept turning her head, and when her head turned so did her body. The drive that was supposed to be straight and orderly wasn't perfect, and Jack knew it. Still, he got them neatly through the second set of gates where Luke was waiting.

Jack could hear Cece and Mandy cheering him on. He checked Luke's face. Luke gave him the wink that said *We know how to do this.* He closed them all inside the pen. The sheep wandered around, looking for a way out. They bumped against Luke but tried to keep their distance from Jack.

The ewe kept banging her nose against the gate. She had the meanest little eyes Jack had ever seen on a sheep. He wondered if she'd been mistreated.

"Separate one from four," said Luke.

One from four. Jack's chance to focus on the ewe, pull her from the others and settle her down.

At a signal from Luke, Jack moved between the ewe and the other sheep. With his eye hard on the ewe, he finally got her still. Two others came around behind. With a single, swift move he sent them back.

He had his two groups.

Luke swung the gate open. Out went the four while Jack held the ewe. Then he let her go. She trotted out like Mary's Little Lamb.

Jack relaxed. Just for a second. But a second was a second too long. The ewe, who wasn't as old or as slow as she looked, bounded away to join the other sheep.

At first Jack's feet wouldn't move. He couldn't believe what had just happened. Then his instincts kicked in and took over. Separating the ewe again, he drove her and the four others across the field.

Holding the gate open, Luke had the strangest look on

his face, a look of complete disbelief. "It's okay, Jack," he said as Jack drove the sheep through. "It's okay, buddy."

But it wasn't. It wasn't okay at all. Jack had let his best friend down, he'd let them all down.

That night he was given a steak, just as if he'd won first place. He couldn't touch it. The small ribbon that was supposed to be big lay on the kitchen counter where Luke had tossed it. Then it made its way onto the desk in Luke's room. Snatching the ugly thing in his teeth, Jack took it out by the trash, dug a deep hole, and buried it.

6

JACK AWOKE IN THE NIGHT to that same mournful howl. He went to the window, pushed the shade up enough to see the familiar field white in the light of the moon. For the remainder of the night, he awoke several times to listen, hearing nothing but Luke's soft breathing as he slept on till morning.

"We'll bring in the sheep tonight," said Olaf, laying a hand on Luke's shoulder. They both looked out at the field covered by a blanket of early morning haze.

Luke had stayed up late reading *The Call of the Wild*. Adventure was on his mind. "Let's leave them," said Luke. "The dogs and I can camp out and guard the sheep."

"And then what we'll have is one tired boy and a bunch of worn-out dogs," said Olaf. "No, we'll bring them in." He mounted his mare. "Come on out when you've finished your lessons. We'll bring the sheep in before dark."

"I can come with you now," said Luke. "We've got to watch extra careful for those coyotes."

"I'll have the dogs with me," said Olaf. "You have school."

Luke made a mule face. "What good is school?"

Olaf turned the mare and trotted off. "Don't let Katrin hear you say that!" he called back over his shoulder.

Jack followed Olaf. It wasn't a school day for him; it was a workday. He reminded the three other dogs of this, and they all set out.

It wasn't until they had crossed the field that Jack saw there were four dogs with him, not three. Jackie had somehow followed without Jack ever seeing her. Either he was slipping, or she was extra sneaky. He pretended to be angry with her, when really he was pleased to see her so keen on learning to herd.

If only she would focus. For a while, she was fine. She did her job diligently, the way the other dogs did theirs. But it wasn't long before he caught her heading for the woods again. He called her back and reprimanded her. She knew he meant business.

So did Olaf. "Take the young one back to the house, Jack," he said.

It was a direct order. Jack had to do what Olaf said. He turned in the direction of home, ordering Jackie to follow.

"No need to come back out, Jack," called Olaf. "Stay home. Rest up. You're not so young anymore, you know."

Jack's heart sank. He didn't understand every word of Olaf's order, but he got the ones that mattered most, the ones that hurt: "rest" and "not young."

All the way back to the house, with Jackie running circles around him, asking him *Why? Why? Why can't I stay?* he heard those words. The same question ran through his own head, though the truth was plain as day: Olaf no longer needed him.

At the house, he left Jackie with her littermates and went inside. Luke, Mandy, and Cece were sitting at the dining room table, their heads bent and their pencils moving. A fan whirred over their heads, stirring the warm air. When Jack put his head on Luke's knee, Luke was surprised. He pushed his chair back and stood. "What's wrong, Jack? Did Olaf send you back to get me? Did you spot a coyote?"

But he could see that Jack was calm. Sad, which wasn't like Jack at all, but he clearly wasn't worried about coyotes.

"Katrin?" said Luke, going into the kitchen, where Katrin was lifting a pan of brownies out of the oven. "Jack came back by himself. Do you think he's all right?"

Katrin came in and knelt beside Jack. She smoothed her hands over his snout and felt his nose. "You okay, Jack?" she said. She looked up at Luke. "His nose is cold.

I don't think there's anything wrong." She lifted Jack's paws, one by one, checking for stickers.

Luke reached for his hat, hanging on a peg by the back door. "I'd better go out and see what's going on."

"Did you finish your essay?"

"Almost."

"Finish it. Then you can go."

"I'll finish my essay tonight. I promise, Katrin!" He was out the door before Katrin could stop him. Jack was right behind.

All the way out to the sheep, Jack worried that he was disobeying Olaf's direct order. But he *had* taken Jackie back to the house, where she was still asleep, curled up with one of her littermates. Jack had rested, too.

And besides, he was Luke's dog. No one else's, not even Olaf's. If Luke said to come, even if he didn't exactly say it, Jack came.

He needn't have worried. The dogs had begun rounding up the sheep and needed all the help they could get. Jack got to work, counting the sheep instinctively, a skill he had learned from a master herder when he was still a pup. He was proud to see that the dogs were skillfully doing their job, though none had mastered the art of counting.

The sheep had come together, grumbling, bumping

sides, wanting to stop at every blade of grass. Jack caught Old Sally's eye. Something was wrong. What was it?

By the time he reached the end of the flock, where Luke and Olaf rode, he knew what it was and his heart sank.

One of the sheep was missing.

He sent a sharp bark up to Luke, who looked down from the saddle. "What's wrong, Jack?"

Jack barked again and made the move that told Luke to follow.

"Something's not right, Olaf," Luke said. "I'm going to check it out."

"Don't be long," said Olaf. "I want to get these sheep in before nightfall."

Jack sniffed the ground, following the strange, acrid scent he'd picked up before in the woods. It had to be coyote, a sick coyote. But Jack knew the smell of coyotes, or thought he did.

He remembered the lone howl in the night that was not a coyote's cry. What was it?

Then he smelled blood, sheep blood, and, stopping only now and then to make sure he had the trail, raced for the woods. Luke kicked Cheyenne into a gallop.

Jack stopped at the tree line, making sure that Luke saw what he saw: a clump of dirty white wool caught in a sticker bush. A coyote had nabbed one of the sheep, and right in broad daylight.

It was not until the sun had climbed halfway up to where it would begin to fall again that the wolf made his move. The alpha canine along with the young one had left. Man and the remaining canines were small figures in the distance.

One of the smaller prey had wandered from its kind. It stood so close now that its rank smell was almost overpowering. The wolf's hunger rose up, demanding to be satisfied. Crouching, he crept forward.

The prey made a strangled, bleating noise as he grabbed it. So thickly furred was this animal that the wolf had trouble locating its jugular. When at last he did, the prey lay limp in his jaws and he dragged it back into the woods.

It was work, this animal. He tore and tore at its fur that stuck in his teeth and made him sneeze. But at last he came to the warm, sweet meat and he feasted like never before.

As night fell, he began to miss his pack again. As good as the furry animal was, nothing could fill the hole the wolf felt in his heart.

7

JACK RAN UP AND DOWN the tree line sniffing bushes, bark, leaves, feathers, and insects dead and alive. A sheep had been picked off on his watch! It *couldn't* be. He'd have known. He'd have felt it. It must have happened while he was gone. He never should have left the sheep to the two-year-olds.

Luke laid a hand on Jack's head as if he could read his thoughts. Sometimes it seemed as if he could. Their shared experience had twinned their minds. But Luke was too young to understand the plight of an aging dog. For every one of Luke's birthdays, Jack added seven. In human years, he was older even than Olaf.

With Jack beside him, Luke turned Cheyenne away from the woods and spurred him into a trot.

"Looks like the coyotes got one of our sheep," said Luke, pulling up alongside Olaf's big mare.

Olaf shook his head, his brow furrowed. "Are you sure?"

Luke gave him the clump of blood-tinged wool he'd pulled from the bush.

Olaf took off his hat and wiped his sweaty forehead with his sleeve. "You sure it happened today?"

"That's what Jack says. It was fresh blood. Anyway, the sheep were all accounted for yesterday."

Curtis or Pinky might have scoffed at this, but not Olaf. "What about this morning?"

"He always counts first thing."

"So the coyotes hit when Jack was gone." Olaf sighed. "I shouldn't have sent him back."

"You hear that, Jack?" said Luke. "You did good."

Jack was relieved but furious with the other dogs. Where were they when the coyotes attacked? What were they doing? Daydreaming?

"What are we going to do, Olaf?" said Luke. "Should we do like Pinky says and carry guns?"

"Gun," said Olaf, holding up a single finger. "We have one gun, and you're not to use it. Besides, what good would a gun have done me today? I never even saw them." He shook his head. "A pack of coyotes carries off one of my flock and I don't even see it happen!"

Luke gave Jack the signal to move the sheep that were starting to mill around as if they were lost. Except for Old Sally, the flock didn't have one whole brain between them. They moved ahead like a slow, muddy river. If they stopped or tried to change direction, one of the dogs immediately set them right.

Any other day, this would have been an easy, peaceful parade. Today Olaf and Luke were anxious to get the sheep to the safety of their pens.

"We need to set some traps. The ones my father used are still in the barn," said Olaf. "I hate the darned things, but we've got to do something."

Luke nodded. "I'll lay the traps out after dinner."

"Good," said Olaf. "You can bait them with some of that venison Curtis sent over."

Luke laughed. "Yes! I hate the stuff. It's tough as cardboard."

"Truth be told," said Olaf, "it's the way your mother cooks it. But don't tell her I said so."

All the way back to the house Jack's mind kept worrying the mystery: some animal, some predator, some *thing* had carried off one of his sheep. If the thing had been a coyote, he'd have settled the question plaguing him. He and the dogs could handle coyotes, and Jack himself would never, for a minute, from this day on, take his eyes off his sheep.

But too many things about this predator were not right, were not coyote. Its strange, acrid scent; its mournful, bone-chilling howl in the night. Whatever it was, Jack knew the way he knew some things that he could never explain: he and this animal would meet.

8

LUKE WAS WASHING the dinner dishes when Cece showed up at the screen door. "Hi!" she said. "Okay if I come in?"

Jack, stretched out on the cool floor under the table, lifted his head. He saw the girl fluffing out her yellow curls and wondered why she always did that. Did she have fleas?

"Sure," said Luke, with a shrug. He pushed open the screen door to let her in.

"I just don't understand algebra," she pouted. "Will you help me with the homework?"

"Uh, okay," said Luke. "I've got to set some traps before it gets dark, that's all. I'll get my book."

"Let's sit in the living room," she said. "On the sofa. These chairs remind me of English class." She made a face.

"Uh, sure," said Luke. He led the way into the living room and went to get his book. When he returned, Cece was sitting in the middle of the sofa. Luke put the book on the coffee table and sat as close to the armrest as he could get.

He reached for the algebra book.

"Oh, let's not start in on that yet," said Cece. "Let's just talk for a while."

"About what?" said Luke. His face was red and his nose was popping beads of sweat.

Jack went over and plopped down on Cece's sandaled feet, making himself as heavy as he could.

"Ouch!" cried Cece. "Get off me." She nudged Jack with her foot.

Jack looked up at Luke, who, he was glad to see, had a big frown on his face.

"Be careful with him," said Luke. "He's a herding dog."

"Sorry!" said Cece, but anybody could tell she didn't really mean it.

Jack let out a big fart.

"Jack!" said Luke, fanning the air. "Not cool!"

Jack got up and left the house. Katrin was weeding the vegetable garden. Olaf was in the barn. Did nobody care about the coyotes? Jack paced around until Cece left and the sun was beginning to set.

At last, Luke came out carrying a plastic bag with strips of meat inside. He went to the barn and began tossing traps into the back of the pickup. When he opened the passenger door, Jack climbed in.

The one good thing you could say about the smelly truck was that it got you out to the sheep faster than anything on four legs. Luke didn't have his license but Olaf let him drive on the ranch. Jack had to admit that it was good to get a ride sometimes.

The sun had dropped behind the trees, casting long shadows across the field. A full moon began to lift like a big white balloon. The first star winked at Jack like the Goat Man used to wink. Jack still missed the Goat Man at times like this. Sometimes he wondered where the old fellow went after he died, and figured there must be a good place for good people like him.

And then he wondered if dogs would be allowed there, and if he would see the Goat Man again.

Luke parked near the trees and he and Jack got out. While Luke baited the traps, Jack sniffed from tree to tree, trying to locate the puzzling urine scent he'd found before.

There it was again, so strong it made him cough. He shook his head and began following the scent trail. The woods grew darker and noisier the farther he went. Birds settling in for the night argued about the best roosting places. Until he came upon them, insects sang their monotonous tune. Then they were as quiet as mice were supposed to be but never really were.

Jack stopped and sniffed the air. He'd lost the scent.

Doubling back to where the light was better, he checked again for tracks he might have missed. Something darted past him to the left, something dark, a dark gray shadow. His hackles rose.

As the sun sent up a final flare, a face appeared between the trees, the wide face of a huge canine, its eyes sharp and wary. The two animals stared at each other for what seemed to Jack like forever. Then the big animal loped off on his huge feet, leaving that strange and unfamiliar scent in the air.

Jack, whose good sense told him that he should be afraid, very afraid, was struck with curiosity. Here again, as in all his past adventures, was something he didn't know, something he needed to know. Were there different breeds of coyote? There were many breeds of dog. Could the same be true of coyote?

At a whistle from Luke, Jack ran back through the woods, the scent of the strange coyote growing ever fainter.

Luke was waiting in the truck with the passenger door open. "Let's head out, Jack," he said. "The traps are all set."

This was one of those times when Jack longed for the trick of human speech. He wanted so badly to share with Luke the mystery of the strange coyote.

He recalled how Jackie went on and on about the dog

with the giant feet. He had thought she was seeing things, or that her imagination might be running away with her. But that wasn't the case. She had seen the huge coyote, and she had come away unharmed.

She was lucky. That time. That animal in the woods was enormous, terrifying in a way that Jack had only known in his dreams.

As they left the woods behind, the strangest feeling came over Jack. It was almost as if he were being drawn back there to something that had not yet happened. Whatever it was would happen soon, and it chilled him to the marrow of his bones.

9

LUKE PULLED THE OLD TRUCK up next to the barn, got out, and came around to open Jack's door. Eager to prove that he wasn't so old, Jack hopped out, giving his joints a jolt that almost made him yelp.

So much for showing off.

Rounding the house, he went to find Olaf, who sometimes had treats in his pocket.

A rattle in the distance stopped him in his tracks. He knew that sound: trash cans. He raced off to where Olaf collected and burned the trash. Olaf wasn't there, but a skinny brown coyote was. With its front paws on the rim of one of the cans, he was about to pull it over. Jack sent out a sharp bark and the coyote dropped to all fours.

Jack expected the young male to retreat as the coyotes often did. But this one stood his ground, desperation in his eyes. He was hungry.

Jack ran at him, hackles raised. The coyote began backing away. Then, as Jack advanced, it changed its mind and charged. Growling, both animals collided in the air, seeking the jugular, their back legs pushing for leverage.

The coyote was stronger than he appeared to be. Jack felt himself being shoved back, the coyote's teeth sinking into his shoulder. Yelping, Jack shook him off. When the coyote got ready to attack again, Jack feinted left, then right, stalling for time. Panting, he tried to regain his strength, but the coyote came at him, forcing him to engage. Growling, they met again, chest to chest.

Through all the growling and snarling, Jack only faintly heard the racket behind him. Olaf, Katrina, and Luke had come running from the house, banging pots and pans and yelling. Then the dogs were everywhere at once, barking and growling, advancing on the coyote, who saw that he was outnumbered and raced off into the night.

Jack's legs were shaking uncontrollably. With Luke on his knees beside him, Jack licked at his wound. "You all right, Jack? Mom, Dad, come look at this. Jack's hurt!"

Katrin knelt and checked the wound. "Let me take a look at this inside," she said. "Don't worry. He's had his rabies shot, and the bite doesn't look deep."

Jack followed Luke to the house, Jackie beside him all the way, hero worship shining in her eyes. Jack knew he should tell her to knock it off. He was no hero. If the others hadn't come, he might not be walking back to the house at all. But her admiration was a welcome antidote for his own worry: he was losing strength, and none of the dogs was ready to take over, not even Jackie.

Katrin, blinking back tears, carefully cleaned Jack's wound. The stuff she used stung and Jack felt like crying, but of course he couldn't.

"If anything happens to Jack, I'll die," said Luke.

Olaf laid a hand on Luke's shoulder. "He'll be fine. He's tougher than he looks."

Jackie's face was a black mask of worry. Jack recognized that look. It came over a collie when a problem presented itself and a solution had to be found. That was why Border collies were so special. They took responsibility for everything. But Jackie was trying to take responsibility for him, which was ridiculous.

He told her to quit it and go to bed.

When Katrin had finished with Jack's wound, he took himself off to bed.

Jack was just drifting off when he heard Luke's voice coming from the kitchen. "I could have shot the stupid coyote and Jack wouldn't have gotten injured!" he cried.

"I don't want to hear any more about it!" bellowed Olaf.

"You can't tell me what to do," said Luke. "I'll get my own gun!"

"Luke!" cried Katrin, as if she'd been slapped.

"I mean it!" said Luke in a voice Jack had never heard before, a man's voice. A chair scraped back. Luke's boots stomped across the wooden floor. The back door slammed so hard the hinges rattled.

10

JACK AWOKE TO DARKNESS when he felt Luke's hand on his back.

"You okay, fella?" said Luke, leaning over the edge of his mattress.

Jack licked Luke's hand. He'd been with the Goat Man again and wanted to get back to his dream world. The Goat Man had been telling Jack about making his "sails of patience," one of those sayings that Jack as a pup had to think a lot about before he understood.

Patience was a lesson he hoped to pass on to Jackie. You couldn't just run off without thinking. Sometimes you had to hold back and use your head first. It was a hard lesson to learn, especially for a Border collie, but it was one that Jackie needed if she was ever to become the lead dog.

The moon lit up the room as if it were morning. "I can't sleep," Luke said. He got up and lowered his window shade. "I'm worried about you. And I'm worried about the sheep. We can't lose any more of them, Jack." He yawned and lay back against his pillow. "Maybe the traps will work." He plumped his pillow and rolled on his side. "If I only had a gun."

Jack didn't like the sound of that. He hated guns. At Pinky's ranch one day, he'd watched Luke, Mandy, and some of the men shooting cans off a fence. Each can was supposed to be a coyote. Blam! Blam! went the guns and Jack had wanted to cover his ears. He'd climbed under the pickup, where at least it was cool and shady.

At the end of the target practice, Pinky and Curtis had sixteen "coyotes" each and Luke had four. Mandy was the best shot of all. Twenty-four dead "coyotes."

Here was a thing that Luke and Mandy, being young, did not understand: killing was ugly. Years ago, Jack had seen the desire for his own death in the eyes of Billy, the owner of that terrible circus, and he had never forgotten it. Killing was a final thing. There was no coming back from it, for the victim or the killer himself.

Then there was killing in self-defense or to save the life of another, which muddied the waters a little. Would he have killed the coyote last night if the coyote had grabbed Jackie?

He would not have hesitated, not for a second.

To Jack's surprise, Luke awoke at the first sounds of morning and climbed into his jeans, shirt, and boots. "Let's check the traps, Jack." He tiptoed past Olaf and

Katrin's bedroom door. Jack followed, his nails clicking against the floor, a thing he couldn't help.

They went as quietly as they could through the kitchen and out the door.

Luke let the pickup roll a little way downhill before starting the engine.

Jack's shoulder ached. He was glad to be off his feet. His wound was probably the reason he was getting a ride today. He and Luke took care of each other that way; they always had.

The sun was busy painting the sky with stripes of color that Luke could probably see better than Jack could. Jack's color sense was keener than most dogs', but still a dog's. That's why the eyes of the big coyote in the woods had startled him so. He had never before seen a canine with eyes like that. They were a lighter color than a dog's eyes or a coyote's, and they were fierce.

Jack and Luke were walking along the perimeter of the woods when they heard the first yelp. Jack's ears went up. Luke stopped in his tracks. Another yelp, high-pitched, desperate. Jack ran in the direction of the sound, Luke on his heels.

A coyote pup was pulling against the steel jaws of a trap, his right front paw caught and bleeding.

"Oh, no!" cried Luke. "It's a puppy!" He dropped to his knees and, with one hand holding the pup down, very carefully opened the trap. The pup snapped at the air trying to bite Luke's hand. Luke held the pup's snout closed and picked him up. "Poor little thing!" he said, holding the squirming pup against his chest. "Let's get that paw fixed. Poor little pup!"

Jack couldn't believe his eyes. Or his ears. Yes, the caught animal was a pup, but it was a predator!

Luke opened the truck door and Jack got in. Then Luke put the pup in the space in front of Jack. "Make him stay," he said.

What was Luke thinking? Was he out of his mind? Jack wasn't a coyote trainer. But he did what he did with any disobedient puppy: he scared the little predator to death by baring his teeth and growling.

The puppy, cowering in the corner, peed all over himself.

11

KATRIN WAS SWEEPING THE STOOP when they drove up.

"Oh, my heavens!" she said when Luke got out with the pup. "Tell me that isn't a coyote."

"It is," said Luke. "And he's hurt." He showed Katrin the puppy's paw, and then there was all this "poor puppy" stuff going on again until Jack, disgusted, went off to see about breakfast.

When Katrin came in and called the vet, Jack was doubly disgusted. She hadn't been this concerned about *him*!

He finished his breakfast and went to his place under the table.

Was it a school day? He couldn't remember. But he was just closing his eyes when he heard Mandy's soft voice: "Oh," she said. "Poor little thing!" The pup, exhausted, had fallen asleep in the cat's bed.

Then Cece chimed in, and for once, Jack was on her side. "You shouldn't have saved that coyote," she said.

"We couldn't let a puppy suffer," said Luke.

"My dad would have," said Cece. "He'd have shot it.

It's just going to grow up and kill your sheep. What are you going to do with it anyway?"

"I don't know," said Luke. "We haven't thought that far yet."

"You haven't thought. Period," said Cece. "Traps are crueler than guns, you know. Just ask my dad. Ask Mandy!"

Luke bit his lip. He glanced over at Mandy.

Mandy, her dark eyes wide, slowly nodded her head.

"I see we have a difference of opinion here," said Katrin, coming in from the bedroom, her hair still damp from her shower and tied in a knot on the top of her head. "This is a great time to study how best to frame arguments for your essays."

Luke groaned. The three kids took their seats around the table.

Sometime later the vet came. He gave the puppy a shot and bandaged his foot. Before he left, he looked at Katrin with grave concern. "You'll never be able to domesticate that coyote, you know."

"Well, we hadn't planned on keeping him," Katrin said.

"Best not let anyone know you have it then," the vet said.

They came after dinner, Pinky, Curtis, and four other men that Jack had seen from time to time.

Olaf opened the door and they stomped into the kitchen, their faces drawn.

"Evening, Katrin. Evening, Olaf," said Curtis Cross, removing his hat. "Evening, Luke."

"Can I get you all some coffee?" said Katrin.

"No, ma'am," said Pinky. "We just came to talk to Olaf."

Olaf got up from the table. "Let's go on outside," he said.

Luke and Jack followed the men out the door.

The moon hung in the dark sky like a ball leaking air. Jack stuck his nose into Luke's cold hand. He could tell that Luke was nervous.

"My daughter came home today with some news that makes me think you might not be as smart as I thought you were, Olaf," said Curtis Cross.

"Oh?" said Olaf. "And what might that be?"

"Something about you saving a coyote." He smiled a crooked smile. He shook his head. "I didn't believe it at first, but my Cece doesn't lie. Tell me she didn't lie."

"She didn't," said Olaf.

Then all the men were talking at once. "What are you thinking, Olaf?"

"You stubborn Swede!"

"Where's the coyote? I'll take care of this myself!"

"Olaf didn't save the pup," said Luke, stepping up. "I did."

"Shush, Luke," said Olaf. "I'll take care of this."

"All I can say," said Curtis Cross, "is if you don't take care of it, one of us will. That coyote will be deader than a picked-off sheep by morning." He turned away and the others did, too, climbing into the front and back of Curtis's truck. The barrels of three rifles on a rack in the rear window gleamed silver in the moonlight.

Olaf sat on the stoop, his head sunk between his shoulder blades.

"What are we going to do?" said Luke.

"Lock the barn and keep the pup in there, I guess. When he's healed, we'll take him back to where we found him. No guarantee the pack will accept him all covered with human smell. But it's the best we can do."

"Do you think I should have left him there?" said Luke.

With a sigh, Olaf got to his feet. "I couldn't have."

Luke shook his head. "Those traps are nasty things, Dad."

"What else can we do?" said Olaf. His eyes told Luke not to answer that, not to bring up the gun again.

When Luke went inside to get the coyote pup, he found him curled up in the cat's bed sound asleep, Jackie beside him. He left them where they were.

Jack did not. He grabbed the cat bed in his teeth and pulled it out from under them. The pups went rolling.

"Okay, okay, Jack. I get it," said Luke. "I get it."

Jack herded the two pups, one yawning, one snarling, into the barn.

"Come on, Jack," said Luke. "You and I are going to gather up those traps before we catch something else we don't need."

12

SOMEONE WAS BANGING on the door. Jack sat up on full alert. It wasn't the front door, or the back one either. The barn door! Somebody was trying to break into the barn, or break it down. The dogs in the barn were barking furiously.

Jack woofed an alarm but Luke didn't awaken. He stuck his nose in Luke's ear. Luke nearly leapt into the air. "Yikes, Jack!" He sat up. "What's going on? What's all that racket?"

He listened. His feet hit the floor. "Dad!"

Luke opened the bedroom door and Jack shot out. He was waiting at the back door when Olaf came in rubbing the sleep out of his eyes.

"Luke?" said Olaf. "What's going on?" He pushed the kitchen curtain back and peered out. "Well, I'll be," he said. "Coyotes."

"I'll get the gun!" said Luke, taking a step toward the fireplace.

Olaf grabbed some pots and pans from the cupboard. "No guns, I said!"

Luke put his hand on the doorknob. "Stay, Jack!"

Stay? Jack whined. He scratched his nails on the linoleum floor and barked once, sharply. Luke knew that bark.

"Do you want to go and get yourself killed? You're already injured. There are too many of them, Jack."

Then Olaf ordered Jack to stay. Jack would have stayed in any case. Never had he disobeyed an order from Luke, but it hurt that he wasn't needed. More of the "old dog" stuff, which was downright demoralizing.

Luke opened the door. He and Olaf went out.

Jack ran to the window and stuck his paws on the windowsill. Bathed in the bright light of the moon were four coyotes: two adults, two half grown. They were milling around, leaping up against the barn door and yipping. One was sniffing underneath the door and had started to dig. Inside the barn, the dogs were going crazy.

When Olaf and Luke started banging pans together and yelling, the coyotes' ears went up and they began to back off. Then they turned and loped away in that strange way they had, as if they were moving both forward and sideways, and as if they had all the time in the world.

Jack heard the shuffle of Katrin's slippers. She came up beside him and looked out the window. "They've come for the little one," she said.

The door opened. Olaf and Luke came in. "See? What did I tell you?" said Olaf. "They're afraid of their own shadow! I wonder why they'd take such a risk though."

"I've read about coyotes," said Katrin. "They're very family-oriented. They'll sacrifice their lives to save one of their own. They want the pup back."

"The coyote that fought Jack wasn't afraid, Dad," said Luke. "It wouldn't hurt to clean that old rifle, just in case."

Olaf shook his head. "I haven't shot a gun in years," he said. "I'd probably shoot my foot off."

"Well, I wouldn't," said Luke. "I'm a pretty good shot. I could take the rifle over to Pinky's and practice."

"Enough about the gun!" said Olaf, his sand-colored eyebrows lowered in a frown.

Luke, his eyes blazing fire, didn't say a word. He just stomped back to his bedroom and slammed the door. Jack had to scratch to be let in.

"He still treats me like I'm ten years old!" cried Luke. "I'll bet Pinky would loan me a rifle if I asked him."

Jack settled into an uneasy sleep. More than any animal on the ranch, man or beast, he wanted peace. He wanted the coyotes to move on to other places and leave his sheep alone. He wanted the other ranchers to mind their own business. He wanted the dogs to guard the sheep as he himself always had, as a Border collie must, with unflagging vigilance. He wanted Luke and Olaf to get along.

He wanted that gun over the fireplace to disappear.

Morning came too soon. Jack awoke when a critter bit his belly. He scratched himself raw trying to track it down.

Luke yawned. "I dreamed about Buck, the dog in *The Call of the Wild*," he said. "Man, that's one great book. You know what happens to Buck, Jack? He gets to be the leader of a pack of wolves! Isn't that cool?"

Jack followed as much of this as he could. He didn't know what wolves were, so he wasn't much impressed. And besides, that darn flea or whatever it was wouldn't get off him.

Today he was going to have a talk with Jackie. All he needed around here was a dog losing her head over a coyote. He followed Luke into the kitchen where Katrin was cooking up a batch of pancakes. She flipped six on a plate for Luke, who dumped a huge lump of butter on top along with half a jug of syrup and dug in.

Jack padded over to his bowl. He took a deep, satisfying sniff of his breakfast. One of the nicer things about being lead dog and Luke's best friend was getting to eat in the kitchen, rather than out in the barn with the rest

of the dogs. The way they carried on! Yapping and pushing each other away from the food. You'd think they
were starving.

He thought about last night's coyotes, so thin you
could see the outline of their ribs. They *were* starving.
Jack knew that when you were really hungry, it was all
you could think about. You took risks you never would
otherwise. He remembered when life had been like that
for him. When he was on the road with his aching stomach, he'd have done almost anything for food. It made
him feel just a little bit sorry for the coyotes. If only they
would leave his sheep alone.

Olaf finished his breakfast and excused himself from
the table. "I've got to check the mare's shoe again," he
said. "She's either got something stuck in there that I
couldn't see last night, or she's going lame. Hope it isn't
that."

"Are you feeling all right?" asked Katrin. "Your face is
flushed." But when she tried to feel Olaf's forehead, he
turned away.

"I'm fine," he said. "I've got work to do."

He went out and closed the door behind him.

Katrin asked Luke if he'd done his biology homework
and Luke said that he had. "I wish I didn't have school
five days a week," he said.

"Well, I guess you could go three days or even two days," said Katrin with a teasing grin. "And about two years longer. How would that be?"

"Bad," said Luke, shaking his head. "Real bad."

The door opened and Olaf stuck his head in. "The coyote pup's gone!"

Luke, Jack, and Katrin raced out to the barn. There they saw the shallow hole the pup had dug under the barn door.

"It must have taken him half the night," said Olaf, scratching the back of his head. "How he did it with that sore foot, I just don't know."

He opened the barn door and Jack ran in.

The second he was inside, he knew: Jackie was gone, too.

The coyote pup didn't dig the hole by himself. He had help.

The wolf was restless. He had staked his territory. He had even found an abandoned cave that sheltered him and, once he found a mate, would provide a measure of safety for his pups. The need to mate drove him now as surely as the need to fill his belly.

He awoke in the light of the waning moon to the sound and smell of canines. He lifted his head, growled low in his throat as the two young canines ran past. The larger of the two he had seen before. She lived among the furry prey.

The small one ran on three legs. Something was wrapped around his right front paw. He belonged to the scavenger pack that had watched the wolf from a distance ever since his coming here. They would wait until he feasted on his kills, then finish the skin and bones he left behind. The wolf allowed this. Unless he was starving, canines were not prey.

But they could be mates. He had known this to happen, this crossbreeding. It had happened in his pack. It had happened in the scavenger pack as well, where two of the young males were crossbred.

The wolf would go well into the depths of his new

territory in search of a mate of his kind before choosing one of the others, but choose he would if he had to. Perhaps this one who guarded the furry prey and who had come into his woods for a second time now. She was fast and fearless. She had the protective instincts that any mate of his must have.

She would not be his first choice, but she would do. He would have to kill off the old alpha male to get her, but it would be no contest. If he decided to take her, the old male was as good as dead.

13

JACK'S STOMACH was tied in knots of worry. He couldn't understand why Jackie would run off with a coyote. Had the stories about his own adventures clouded her judgment?

She was tenderhearted, a trait that Jack tried to see as a failing but could not. She had probably left with the idea, the *foolish* idea, that she could protect the puppy. That she could guide him back to his family.

But coyotes, even coyote pups, had homing instincts. Surely they did. The pup would have found his way back. But Jackie could not have known that.

How would the coyotes react when they saw her? They would see her as enemy, one of those who had stolen their pup. They would attack to drive her away, or in their anger injure her.

Or worse.

And what of the huge coyote? Was he their leader? If so, Jack knew he was no match for a beast that size. Even in his youth he was not. But he would save Jackie if he could. At the very least he would hold the coyote off until she could get away.

Why were they all just standing around!

But Katrin and Olaf were busy talking loudly. Katrin laid her hand on Olaf's forehead. "You're burning up!" she said. "No work for you today."

"But—"

"No argument, mister," said Katrin.

"Yeah, Dad," said Luke. "Go back to bed. Jack and I can handle things."

Olaf's whole face pinched in frustration. He frowned at his wife, then he frowned at Luke. "You be careful," he said.

"Don't worry, Dad. We're always careful."

Behind the wheel of the truck, Luke reached up to set his hat right and Jack nudged his arm.

"Okay! Okay, Jack! We're going!" Luke cranked the key. The old engine caught and roared into life.

They bumped out over the fields toward the woods, darker and more threatening than they had ever looked. Even the sun refused to come out from behind the clouds, as if it were afraid to see what might happen.

Were they too late? Was Jackie's short life on earth already over? Jack could not bear to think it, but think he did. He'd let that pup deeper into his heart than any of the others. He should have known better.

It was a longer trip than it had ever been, but at last the truck came to a stop. In his eagerness to begin the search, Jack nearly leapt out the window. Then he thought better of it. His brain was ready for anything, but his body no longer was. He waited until Luke opened the door and climbed down.

They went along the edge of the woods, Luke calling for Jackie, Jack checking every twig, every leaf for Jackie's scent.

There! No. Not hers, *theirs*. Coyotes'. Jack bounded into the trees, stopping only to sniff and then take off again.

"Wait, Jack!" called Luke. But except for the occasional sniff to guide him, Jack could not slow down.

The mingled scent of coyote deepened as the woods grew denser and noisier. Overhead a hawk screamed. Crows quarreled. Insects sang and buzzed, snakes slithered through the leaves. Jack's ears fought to keep out every other sound but the huff of canines.

There!

He stopped again.

There was that other scent, the one that somehow wasn't right.

Jack zigzagged back and forth, losing one scent, still not Jackie's, and gaining another.

And then, just like that, like smoke into thin air, the trail went cold.

Jack stopped. He retraced his steps, picked up a scent, searched the area in widening circles, and then nothing. The pack had disappeared.

What had gone wrong? Coyotes couldn't fly, and yet they were gone. He had taken a wrong turn somewhere. He thought he was smelling coyote when he wasn't.

And what if all that scent was from another pack? A different family than the pup's? Then Jackie could be anywhere in these woods, or in the hills beyond, and he had lost her for good.

He barked again, his sharpest call, the one that meant business, the one that meant *Now!*, but only his echo returned.

With Luke behind him, Jack retraced his steps. He searched the perimeter of the woods again, back and forth, until he caught the acrid odor, the one that still bewildered him.

"We've got to get home, Jack," said Luke at last. "Bertha's gonna kick us from here to Oregon if we don't get her milked."

Jack balked. He set his feet. He barked once, sharply.

Luke frowned. He turned toward the truck. "Jack," he said quietly. "Come."

A direct order.

As angry as he'd ever been in his life, Jack slowly followed Luke back to the truck. Luke was right. There was work to be done. The animals needed to be fed, the sheep had to be herded out. He would spend the day as he always did, making sure the sheep were safe. It was his job, his first responsibility.

But what about Jackie? He had to get back to these woods and find her. His mind began inventing ways that he could slip away without Luke knowing. Where did his greatest responsibility lie anyway? With Luke, his handler and best friend, or with Jackie, his granddaughter?

He hated this dilemma for which there was no right answer. His responsibility lay with both of them, but still he had to choose.

As they headed back to the house, Jack thought about his dad, who had passed on the strict Border collie code: the sheep would always depend on him and him alone. They were his first and only duty. If he wavered in his purpose, a life could be lost.

He had passed that same tradition on to Jackie, and she seemed to be listening. But what exactly had she heard? What if she took him to mean the value of all animal life, even coyote life?

How could you explain that some lives were worth more than others? And were they? Olaf didn't think so and neither did Katrin. It was a perplexing thing, this idea. It made sense to Jack that whoever had made him made all the animals, and that the creator would be someone like Olaf. Someone who loved all of his creatures.

But it made no sense at all that he could get this old and still not know things. He wished he could ask his dad if herding sheep was enough to be the whole purpose of a collie's life, or if there was something bigger, more important. But he knew what his father would say. A collie's duty was everything.

And the Goat Man? What would he say?

Love. The Goat Man would say the bigger purpose was love. But could that be right? Could love be more important than duty?

All the way home, Jack's mind ran back and forth, from love to duty, from duty back to love. From the Border collie code to the Goat Man's philosophy. From herding sheep to protecting his own kin.

Until now he had always been able to do both. He had never had to choose between duty and love, and he couldn't now.

Love. Bertha the kicking cow didn't know the

meaning of the word. When Luke sat down to milk her, Jack, expecting a hoof to strike out, got his face slapped hard by her big, fat, smelly tail.

If there was something lower on the scale of animal life than sheep, this cow was surely it.

The wolf knew, without knowing how he knew, that his time on earth was short. Only his senses drove him now, not his brain, which was more and more often confused. A female wolf that he had tracked turned out to be a coyote, and then a ghostly shape, and then nothing at all. He would awaken in the night certain that he was in the place of his birth, among his kind, and that certainty, too, would fade.

He roused himself from his resting place in the cave. He would go to where he knew the canine scavengers gathered and watch them. Far inferior to wolves, there was still much about them to admire. Cleverness, keen senses, loyalty to their kind. He would choose one for his mate. He could not put this off much longer.

He came near, watching from a distance, surprised to see the young canine who ran with the sheep among them. She did not feed as the others did on the animal carcass, though she watched with hungry eyes. She was wary and seemed to know her place.

The pup she had come with into the woods ignored her now. When she took a step toward the pup, he broke from the feed and, growling, bared his bloody teeth. She backed off, then turned from the pack.

The wolf followed her, stopping when she stopped, changing direction when she did. He sensed that she was lost, or that her mind was troubled in some way. When she turned and headed back in his direction, all he had to do was wait.

The little female was right for him, he knew that now. He would make her his mate.

She stopped and, sniffing the air, began to turn again. That was when he made a soft sound deep in his throat. Seeing him, she froze.

He went to her, touched her nose with his, felt her trembling run straight through his own body. When she whimpered, he made that soft sound again. He sniffed her ears, her neck. Every ounce of her wanted to bolt and run, he could feel it, but fear held her in place.

Had one of the canines already mated with her? Was he too late?

From the field, not far away, came the sound of a sharp, urgent bark. The female turned her head and was about to answer when the wolf growled a warning. She whimpered and backed away. He moved with her, and when she turned and ran, he followed, one of his long lopes equal to four of hers. He loped behind, and when she broke into the field, he was beside her.

Four dogs came at him at a dead run. He let the female dash away and crouched, ready to fight.

14

"JACK! STOP! IT'S A—"

Whatever else Luke said was lost as Jack raced straight for the huge coyote. Beside Jack, matching him stride for stride, was Sarge. Casey and Freckles were right behind. Jack barely had time to register his relief that Jackie was alive before they circled the coyote, growling and barking.

In a half crouch, ready to spring, the coyote stood his ground. Foam dribbled from his jaws and his eyes were dull. Jack sensed they were facing a sick animal and hesitated.

But Sarge did not. Without waiting for a signal from Jack, Sarge lunged for the coyote, who took no time at all pinning him down.

"No! Sarge!" Luke cried.

It was over in seconds and the coyote, his muzzle pink with foam and Sarge's blood, turned toward the others. He was panting hard.

Casey and Freckles, barking furiously, kept their distance. They had seen how fast their friend had been taken down. The coyote turned his big head toward Jack and Jack dug in, ready to fight.

"Back off, Jack!" cried Luke. "He'll kill you!"

Cheyenne whinnied and pranced in fear.

The coyote shook his head, shook it again. Then his eyes cleared, and for a long moment, he looked straight at Jack, into Jack's eyes. Everything went still—the wind, the trees, even Cheyenne. Everything that breathed, waited.

Then the big coyote turned and loped off into the woods.

Luke dropped to his knees and laid his hand on Sarge's side. "He's gone. Sarge is gone." Luke stayed there on his knees for the longest time, and when he got up his face was wet with tears. "That was a wolf, Jack! A *rabid* wolf. You're lucky he didn't kill all four of you."

Wolf. So it wasn't a coyote. Whatever it was called, this one was the stuff of nightmares. The speed with which he'd killed Sarge was terrifying, and Jack knew that he would have been next. Why the wolf didn't go ahead and kill him was mystifying.

Jack touched Sarge's nose with his own. He looked into Sarge's lifeless eyes. It was so hard to believe that his loyal friend was gone, that he wouldn't be coming when Jack called him. Jack wanted to tell him what a good dog he'd always been, what a good friend he was, but it was too late for that.

Luke lifted Sarge's lifeless body and draped it over the saddle. Taking Cheyenne's reins in hand, he began walking home.

"Let's get the sheep in fast, Jack," he said. "Until we deal with that wolf, we're keeping them penned."

Jack raced toward the sheep, who seemed to have missed the whole show, meandering slowly in their usual way. And then he saw why. Jackie had kept them together all by herself, racing from one end of the flock to the other, seeming to be everywhere at once.

How was it that he could be so angry with her one moment and so proud the next?

Casey and Freckles lagged behind. Like Jack, they couldn't seem to believe that their friend was not coming to help round up the sheep. Until Jack barked a sharp order, they stood watching Sarge going home for the last time.

Katrin looked up from the vegetable patch she was weeding and got to her feet. "Back so soon?" she said. Then she saw Sarge's body draped across Luke's saddle and her eyes filled with tears. "No," she said. "Oh, no, no, no." She gathered Luke into her arms. "What happened? What happened to Sarge?"

Jack could see on Luke's face that he didn't want to tell her about the wolf. Luke didn't want his mom to worry, that was for sure. But there was something else, too. Jack chewed on that thought like a bone. He didn't like not knowing what his best friend was thinking.

Luke told her what happened, keeping the scariest parts to himself.

"A wolf!" cried Katrin. "Are you sure? Oh, Luke! If Olaf weren't sick—no, we've got to call Curtis. Do not under any circumstances go near the woods."

Luke frowned.

"Luke!" she said, with a fierceness in her eyes that she rarely had. "Do you hear me?"

Jack had his answer. Luke wanted to take care of that wolf himself.

"I hear you," Luke said.

15

"DAD!" cried Luke, barging through the screen door into the kitchen.

"Hush!" said Katrin. "Your father is sick. Please keep your voice down."

"But—"

"Luke, please. I'll call Curtis. I can't have you disturbing your father."

Luke and Jack watched her carry a glass of water into the bedroom and close the door behind her.

Luke went straight for the rifle that hung over the fireplace. Lifting it down, he dusted it with the hem of his T-shirt. "No time to break it down and clean it," he said. He wiped the sweat off his forehead with the back of his wrist. "I'll bet we couldn't find one bullet around here if we turned the whole place upside down!" He opened a drawer and rummaged through it.

Jack's eyes went from Luke's face to the gun and back again. He didn't like seeing Luke with the gun in his hands. He had heard the air crack with the angry sound of fire. He had seen cans and bottles explode. What a gun could do to his best friend was more than he wanted to know.

He nudged Luke's leg. He looked up into his eyes.

"Don't worry, Jack. I'll be careful." Luke laid his hand on Jack's head for a second before opening another drawer. He ran his hand across the topmost shelf of the bookcase.

"Aha!" he said. "Here they are." He leaned the gun against the chair and opened a red cardboard box.

Jack looked at the gun, then at Luke, and back at the gun. For all he knew, the thing could jump up and shoot itself.

Luke slipped some bullets from the box into his pocket. "Come on, Jack," he said. "We've got work to do."

They left the house, Luke closing the door quietly behind them. For a moment, he stood looking across the field toward the Cross ranch. Casey, Jackie, and Freckles milled around, waiting for orders. "Maybe we should get Mr. Cross," Luke said. "Or Pinky."

Frowning, he turned on his heel and strode toward the truck. "Nah. They think we can't take care of stuff on our own, but we can. Dad said we could. Right, Jack?"

Jack's answering bark was less convincing than he meant it to be. Luke wasn't exactly right. The wolf wasn't Luke's job, it was Jack's. He and the dogs should have taken that wolf down when they had the chance. Now Luke was in the middle of it, Luke and the gun that Olaf never wanted him to have.

Jack told the dogs to stay behind and keep an eye on the sheep. He couldn't have them mixed up in this.

Casey and Freckles headed for the pens. After some begging and a sharp order from Jack, Jackie turned and followed them. She had yet to be punished for running off with the coyote pup, and seemed to know she was testing the limits of her grandfather's patience.

Luke laid the gun in the bed of the truck and opened the door for Jack to climb in. They rolled a good long way before Luke finally started up the truck.

"I couldn't just wait around, Jack," Luke said, as if Jack had asked him why they were going after the wolf alone. "Dad's sick. Who knows how long until Curtis gets here. We can take care of that wolf, Jack. You and me."

Jack stuck his snout out the window and asked the wind to blow his worries away. He didn't want to see that wolf again, not dead and for sure not alive.

Why was Luke being so stubborn? Why did he have to go after the wolf by himself? Curtis Cross and Pinky were better shots than he was. Luke should wait for one of them.

But there was a whole part of Jack that understood

Luke as well as he understood himself. Like his father and Old Dex had told Jack from the beginning, guarding the sheep was his responsibility and his alone. And Luke took responsibility for *everything*. Not only for the sheep, but for the whole ranch.

Olaf didn't ask him to. It was just what Luke himself believed. He believed what Jack believed. You didn't expect anybody else to do your job for you. No matter how hard or how dangerous, you went out and took care of things yourself.

16

WHEN THE TRUCK came to a stop and the engine was still, all the sounds of nature returned. Jack waited impatiently for Luke to let him out. Then they started for the woods, Luke carrying Olaf's rifle as if it were his own.

Jack heard hoofbeats in the distance and saw Curtis Cross on his big black gelding, galloping straight toward them. Clouds of dust blew up in his wake.

Luke spun around. "Oh, no!"

Curtis Cross pulled the reins and the big horse slowed to a stop. He frowned down at Luke. His frown deepened as he took in Olaf's gun. "Your mother called. Said there was a wolf out here. What are you thinking, boy?" said Curtis Cross as the gelding pranced and snorted.

Luke was about to answer when another horse appeared on the horizon. Mandy's pinto came galloping toward them for all she was worth. Mandy's rifle in its scabbard bounced against the pinto's side. "Whoa! Whoa, Banner!" she said, and trotted up beside her father.

"Mandy?" said Luke. "What are you doing here?"

"Mom said you needed help. That you were all alone and . . ." She shrugged.

Curtis Cross raised an eyebrow. "Mandy here's the best shot around. You need help and we're here to make sure nobody gets hurt."

"Thanks, but we don't need any help," said Luke in a deep, firm voice. "Jack and I can handle it."

Curtis Cross lowered his bushy eyebrows. "And I can handle a charging rhino with a slingshot. Don't be a fool, Luke. Leave the truck here. You can ride with me."

Luke pinched his lips together. Then he stomped over to the pinto and climbed into the saddle behind Mandy. Jack raced to keep up as the horses headed for the woods.

Even though he had always taken Luke's side, Jack had been relieved to see their neighbors. This was no coyote they were hunting, it was the biggest, meanest canine Jack had ever seen.

Jack would keep an eye on their friends, but Luke was his first priority. Jack would hurl himself between the wolf and Luke in the blink of an eye if he had to. He didn't want to, but as the woods loomed ever closer, he knew that he would.

Curtis Cross, in the lead, raised his hand. "Hold up! We'll leave the horses here and go in with the rifles."

Clutching Olaf's rifle, Luke dismounted, followed by Mandy. Luke's face was knotted up with anger and worry. Then his face cleared, and maybe his mind as well, because he called ahead to Curtis Cross.

Curtis Cross turned and waited for Luke to catch up. He looked at the woods as if he could see into them. "I want you both to stay behind me. And you"—he pointed at Luke—"keep the safety on that danged rifle. Mandy knows better, but you I don't know about. I don't want to get shot in the back."

Luke scowled but Jack saw his eyes go to Olaf's gun. Jack hoped Luke knew what a safety was because Jack sure didn't.

Curtis Cross strode toward the woods, his rifle in the crook of his arm.

"Don't let my dad get to you," said Mandy. "He's just worried, that's all."

"He's got a right to be," said Luke. Then he stopped and frowned at Mandy. "Look," he said. "You shouldn't be out here."

A sharp look came into Mandy's brown eyes. "Why not?"

"Because . . . Because. I don't know—Because you're a *girl*!"

"Luke Nielson! I thought you were smarter than that. You really think that girls aren't as good as boys?"

"I didn't say that!" cried Luke. "I just meant, you know, as strong . . ."

"And brave and smart, too, I suppose!" She shook her head and walked on ahead.

"Mandy, *hey*!"

"Hay is for horses, doofus," she said. "Come on, the big bad wolf is waiting."

Luke's mouth dropped open. No words came out. Then he knelt and laid his hand on Jack's head. "Stay with the horses, Jack," he said.

With the horses? What was Luke thinking? Jack barked NO. But he knew an order when he heard one.

"Please let me come," he whined.

His last try was a pitiful yip.

"Stay," said Luke softly. "You saw what happened to Sarge." He ruffled Jack's neck fur. "I can't lose you, buddy."

"But I don't want to lose *you*!" said Jack with his eyes and every cell of his body.

Jack watched Luke running to catch up with Curtis and Mandy Cross. His feet wanted to race ahead so badly they itched. He yipped again, even though he knew it was too late and Luke would not hear him.

It wasn't fair. He was back here with the horses because he was old, that's all, and it just wasn't fair.

17

AS THE HORSES GRAZED PEACEFULLY on the dry grass, Jack began to circle them. Not because he cared about the horses one way or another, but only because he'd been ordered to. It was his job and he always did his job well.

His mind went in circles, too. How could he get himself to where he needed to be without disobeying a direct order?

Would Luke forgive him if, just this once, he disobeyed?

Of course he would. But he would never trust Jack again. And Jack would not blame him. Trust had been at the heart of all Jack's father's lessons. If a dog could not be trusted to do his duty, what good was he to anyone? And if that dog was a Border collie and proved he could not be trusted? Then he would let down all the collies that came before him as well as all those that he sired.

Trust was no small thing.

Deep in thought, Jack did not realize at first how big his circle had become. In their grazing, the horses were straying from each other. The gelding moved steadily in the direction of home, while Banner ambled her way toward the woods.

Now here was a dilemma if ever there was one: Jack was to stay with the horses, but which one? For a while, he ran between them, back and forth. When he tried to herd them, the gelding's back hoof narrowly missed his head. Edging ever closer to the trees, Banner just ignored him.

Jack raised his head, sniffed the air, and listened. The woods were quiet, ominously quiet. What if it was already too late and the wolf had taken them all down? The speed with which the beast had killed Sarge had proved that even a sick wolf was stronger and faster than the fittest dog.

And if that was so, what chance would a mere human have?

He nudged Banner and she moved a step back.

He ran to the woods and sniffed along the perimeter. Rotting leaves, animal urine, bird droppings, bug and snake trails, coyote. He stopped and sniffed again.

Banner nickered and Jack looked up as she shook her mane. She had come as far as the trees. He barked an order that she ignored.

Jack looked away from her straight into a pair of watchful eyes. His hackles rose. His heart began to race.

The wolf didn't move. He just stared at Jack as if—Jack couldn't really tell—as if he wanted to *know* him.

A growl arose in Jack's throat. He swallowed it and stared back at the wolf, who hadn't moved as much as a hair. A gust of wind blew in and stirred the dust, and when it was gone so was the wolf.

Jack barked a sharp warning into the woods. If Luke heard his bark, he would come running. Jack could only hope that Luke would be ready for the wolf and that Curtis and Mandy Cross would be with him. Meanwhile, he would not let down his guard.

Then Banner, for some silly reason, snorted and rose up on her back hooves. A snake slithered past. Before Jack could form his next thought, a streak of gray flew through the air, and the wolf was on Banner's back. She whipped around and around trying to shake it off, but the wolf clung to her mane with his teeth. Whinnying frantically, Banner rose up and pawed the air, but the wolf clung, all claws and teeth. Jack, trying to stay clear of Banner's hooves, raced in and out, barking and snarling.

An explosion came out of the trees and Curtis Cross appeared, his glasses askew and his rifle raised. Luke dropped Olaf's rifle as Mandy raised hers. Before she could get off a shot, the wolf leapt off Banner and streaked into the woods. Banner fell to her knees, breathing hard.

Mandy dropped her rifle. She knelt, throwing her arms around Banner's neck. "Dad!" she cried. "She's hurt!"

As Banner whinnied and shook her head, Curtis grabbed her reins and tried to ease her up. "There now," he said. "There now."

"Daddy! That wolf! There was foam in his mouth! He's rabid!"

Curtis Cross put his other arm around his daughter. "I know, honey."

As father and daughter tended to the horse, Jack and Luke remained on guard. But the woods had swallowed up the wolf.

He was gone as if he had never been.

18

"I'LL HAVE TO GET THE TRAILER," said Curtis
Cross. "Come with me, Mandy."

Mandy shook her head. "I'm staying here with Banner," she said.

Her father took a deep breath and let it out his nose.
He turned to Luke. "Can I trust you to use that gun if you
need to?"

"Yes, sir," said Luke, standing soldier straight.

"All right then. I'll be back in a flash." He mounted
the gelding and took off at a gallop in the direction of
his ranch.

Mandy stayed behind, her head on Banner's neck, tears
running into the little mare's mane. "You'll be okay,
Banner. You'll be okay, baby."

But Jack could see that she didn't believe it, and neither did Banner. Her eyes rolled, and when she tried to
get to her feet, she stumbled and went down again.

Luke stood guard, watching the woods, rifle ready.
Jack stood at his side. With her arms around Banner,
Mandy sobbed her heart out.

The woods that had gone silent were starting up again. Life went on for all the creatures there, even the wolf. Jack hated the fear that kept him glued to Luke's side. He could tell himself that he was protecting Luke, and he was, but it was more than that. He knew he could not take the wolf down. The animal was too strong, too quick. He was sick, and still he was stronger and faster than any dog Jack had ever known.

At last they saw the Cross pickup coming over the rise, pulling a horse trailer.

Banner balked going into the trailer, but they finally got her loaded.

Luke grabbed Mandy's hand as she was about to climb into her father's truck. "I'm sorry, Mandy," he said. "It was my fault all this happened. If only I'd—"

"No way, Luke," said Mandy, tears still clinging to her eyelashes. "Dad and I should have found that wolf and shot it, but we didn't."

"But I should have just waited for you!"

"Yes, Luke," said Curtis Cross. "You should have. But that's all water under the bridge now. We've got to get Banner home as fast as we can. The vet's on his way."

"Yes, sir," said Luke, blinking back tears.

"Get yourself home. We'll come back with a hunting party first thing in the morning and take care of that wolf."

When the truck was out of sight, Luke turned to Jack. "Let's get him, Jack," he said, tightening his grip on the rifle. "Let's get that wolf." He turned and strode toward the woods.

Jack stood his ground. The bark he gave Luke was one he used on errant sheep or dogs who wouldn't mind. "Come back here," it said.

Luke ignored him.

Jack barked again. Luke had no business going after that beast by himself, gun or no gun. But Jack knew that, along with Olaf's rifle, Luke carried a load of guilt and sorrow. He blamed himself for Sarge's death, the death of the sheep, and for what had just happened to Banner. He didn't know what to do with his guilt but try to blast it away. He kept walking ahead, and Jack had no choice but to follow him.

They neared the trees, Jack's heart hammering, and he thought for a minute that Luke was going to go charging right in. But he didn't. He was scared, too. Jack could smell it on him.

Luke took a deep breath. He laid his rifle against the felled trees he and Olaf had stacked last spring. Leaning back, he rested for a bit, and Jack thought he might be changing his mind. But his eyes were still clouded in thought. Turning, he gave the logs a good, hard kick with the heel of his boot. "My fault!" he said. "*My fault.*"

A creak, then a crack, and the topmost log seemed to yawn and stretch. The ones beneath groaned and shifted. Down came the huge log, bouncing free. Before Luke could leap away, he was knocked to the ground, his left leg pinned under a log as big around and heavy as Curtis Cross. When he tried to move his leg, Luke screamed. "Jack! Get Dad!"

How could Jack leave? He couldn't leave Luke, but he had to get help. There was no way they could move that log.

Reluctantly, he turned toward home and there was Jackie, racing toward them as if she'd been called. He stopped her with a sharp bark. She cocked her head. "Get home!" he said. "Now! Tell Olaf to come."

Jackie's eyes got wide. Then her tail went rigid and her hackles rose.

"Jack! Watch it!" cried Luke. "It's the wolf." He raised his rifle as the wolf came straight for them.

"Help!" cried Luke. "Somebody help!" The barrel of his rifle shook as he aimed for the wolf. His shot went wide.

Jack moved between the wolf and Luke faster than he'd ever moved before. This was his best friend, the person he loved more than life itself. His answer to what was most important. Not love *or* duty, but both.

As he and the wolf met chest to chest, Jack felt as if

he'd hit a solid brick wall. He could not move it, not with every ounce of his strength and will and might. He could only hope to hold the wolf off until help came. If the beast killed him, he'd kill Jackie and Luke as well.

From within the blood and bones and sinews of his body Jack pulled strength he never knew he had, a young dog's strength. But even as a young dog, he'd have been no match for this wolf, whose sharp teeth snapped as they went for Jack's neck and missed.

Jackie ran in circles around them, diving in for a nip at the wolf's hind legs, her barks high-pitched and frantic. As the wolf turned toward Jackie, Jack leapt at him. Chest to chest again, they snarled and snapped, the wolf pushing Jack against his weakening back legs.

Jack knew it would all be over in minutes unless he did something else. But what?

He was a sheep dog, born and bred. He dropped and feinted right. The wolf hesitated in surprise. When he attacked again, Jack dodged and feinted left.

Jack was breathing hard, but so was the wolf. Foam dripped from his jaws. His eyes looked crazed, unfocused. Jack saw him gather himself for a final attack. Jack had to think his way out of this.

The idea came to him as a gift from that long-ago circus. Jack stood his ground and, when the wolf flew at him, did a flip right over his back. The confused wolf turned and Jack flipped over him the other way.

Jack wondered how long he could keep this up when Jackie grabbed the wolf's tail. The wolf lunged for Jackie, and Jack went for him, landing on the wolf's back, grabbing his neck fur and hanging on with all his might. The wolf's blood, hot and thick, seeped into his mouth.

The wolf spun left and right, trying to shake Jack off his back and Jackie off his tail. Jack could hear the wolf's ragged breathing as he tired. Jack sank his nails deep into the wolf's back as the wolf turned this way and that, Jackie flinging around at the end of the wolf's tail like it was one of her chew toys. From somewhere that seemed very far away, Jack heard Luke calling his name, crying. Exhausted and desperate, Jack told himself to hold on. All he had to do, if it was the last good act of his life, was to hold on.

At last the wolf stumbled and went down. Breathing hard, foam dripping from his tongue, he did not move. The fight was over.

Jack leapt off him. He ordered Jackie to let go of the wolf's tail. Backing off, they watched the wolf slowly get to his feet, shaking his head as if there was something inside that he needed to be rid of.

Jack crouched at the ready. Jackie did the same.

"Let him go!" cried Luke. "Let him go, Jack!"

They all watched the wolf, without a backward glance, lope off into the woods.

Luke shot three times into the air.

Jack ran to Luke, licked his face and hands.

Luke reached up and put his arms around Jack, sobbing into his fur. "I thought he would kill you, Jack."

Jackie touched Jack's nose. "I did good, right?"

"You did good, Jackie," he said.

Curtis and Pinky rode in like a posse. With one big man at each end, they lifted the log off Luke's leg. Luke yelped as they got him to his feet.

Curtis ran his hand over Luke's leg. "Broken," he said. "Go easy with him."

"The wolf came back," Luke said. "That's why I sent up a signal. Jack fought him off."

Curtis Cross gave Jack an appraising look. "Didn't know you still had it in you, old fella," he said.

"I'll go in after that wolf," said Pinky, clutching his rifle.

"No need," said Curtis Cross. "It's getting dark. We'll alert all the folks and come back tomorrow. Even if we don't find him, he'll be dead in a week, maybe sooner. Rabies is quick."

"We'll watch for him," said Luke, grimacing as Curtis Cross laid him in the bed of Olaf's truck. "Jack and me."

"Right!" said Curtis Cross with a smirk. "And I'll do a jig with a grizzly bear."

19

LUKE SAT ON THE SOFA with his leg in a cast and resting on a pillow. Katrin handed him two aspirins and water to swallow them with. She and Olaf had been so angry with Luke they could hardly speak. Luke said at least a hundred "I'm sorrys" and meant every one. Now the house was calm again.

Cece knelt to write her name on Luke's cast.

"Poor Luke," she said. "If my daddy had been there when that wolf came back, he'd have shot him right between the eyes."

Jack stretched himself out under Luke's extended leg. He knew what Luke was thinking: Curtis Cross had had his chance to kill the wolf and missed. From what Luke had told him, it was one thing to shoot a can sitting on a fence and another to shoot an animal in motion.

"The dogs took that wolf on," said Luke. "You should have seen them! He didn't have a chance."

"Which dogs?" said Cece. "Dad said Jackie was out there, but she's still a pup."

"That was my fault," said Katrin, coming in from the

kitchen with a plate of cookies. "She got the door open somehow and let herself out."

"She wants to be with Jack, wherever he goes," said Luke.

Jack knew it was more than that. For some reason, Jackie had decided that it was her duty to protect him. He'd have to talk to her again. She loved him, and that was all well and good, but he was not her responsibility. Maybe she'd have a better understanding since the fight with the wolf that he could take care of himself.

She should be punished for breaking the rules, like Luke, who was grounded for a month, but how could he punish her when she'd helped save his life? Her duty had been to follow his orders, but she couldn't. Not when someone she loved was in danger.

Duty and love. Jackie had known all along that they were the same.

Jack felt good about fighting off the wolf, proud of himself. Maybe he wasn't as old as he thought. Maybe he didn't have to retire, not yet. Maybe he still had some good years left in his old body after all.

He'd have liked to hear more about how great he and Jackie had been, but Luke and Mandy were talking about Banner now. Jack was glad to hear that she was going to be all right. She'd had her rabies shot, which was good, because not every horse got them. In all the fuss, Jack had forgotten to heap the usual blame upon himself for not protecting her.

He did that now.

With the world so filled with animals of every kind in need of protection, how could he even think about retiring? He was a Border collie. It was his job to see that his world ran in a safe and orderly manner. Maybe he wasn't in charge of everything, but today? Today he was feeling like Top Dog, all right. He was completely and absolutely in charge. Nothing could ruffle him. He yawned and closed his eyes. It was time for a long nap.

The wolf ran as long as his legs allowed. Then he loped. Then he slowed to a walk. He stopped for a time, exhausted and confused, his big head hanging. Survival was a voice deep in his being that pushed him to move, to breathe. Lifting his head, he forced his legs on. Shelter. He needed the shelter of his cave.

The woods looked unfamiliar to him now, as if he had entered them for the first time. Trees leaned in, pressing him down. The sky darkened. There was no light to go by, no moon.

A cold wind arose, swirling leaves into the shapes of living things. What was this place? Where was his cave?

The fear in his belly would not leave him. Not fear of the fierce little dogs, nor fear of the humans with their sound-shattering sticks. The wolf's fear was deeper and more painful than that. He knew now that he would never mate. There would be no pups to carry on after him, no pack of his own. He would die with no one to mourn or remember him.

He came to a stop, breathing hard. He shook his head several times. The fear and confusion remained. He was weak. Had he always been? Had his pack known that about him? Was that why he was sent away?

No. There was a time—he remembered now—a time when he was strong, confident, virile. A wolf in his prime. He had run with boundless energy. The strong blood of his pack ran through him and gave him courage.

Then came the bite of the big rodent and the course of his life changed forever.

As night crept in, the air grew sharp with cold. The wolf retraced his steps until at last he spotted the cave he had passed without knowing. His last bit of strength took him up the small rise and he crawled into the cave. He would rest now, and in the morning—

There would be no morning. He knew that now. But how? What made him so sure? Every living thing must feel its own end, he thought. He was nothing special. He had no special powers.

This knowing: was it a gift or a curse?

He slept for a time and awoke. Or thought that he awoke. It was hard to tell. Then he heard it. A howl or a call. He lifted his snout and tried to answer but could not.

Shapes rose around him, shadows, spirits, at once strange and familiar. The smells of his infancy returned,

of his mother, of her warmth, her warm fur. They closed
in around him as one, his pack, and he was comforted. He
could hear their soft breathing. He lifted his head and
howled his joy. At last, he was not alone. They were taking
him home.

Acknowledgments

This little book came through Frances Foster's magical hands with Susan Dobinick at her side. My gratitude to these two shepherds and to Gwen Dandridge, who eagerly bounced off my ideas and made them better. Also thanks to the rest of my excellent writing group, Kim, Lori, and Sherrie, for their ongoing encouragement and support. Carol Hiles came up with the title in the middle of our pool workout, and it was perfect. My gratitude for every child who asked for this sequel. And thanks always to my first editor and love, Jack Hobbs.